fool's gold

color me consumed

melody carlson

Discipleship Inside Out™

NavPress is the publishing ministry of The Navigators, an international Christian organization and leader in personal spiritual development. NavPress is committed to helping people grow spiritually and enjoy lives of meaning and hope through personal and group resources that are biblically rooted, culturally relevant, and highly practical.

For a free catalog go to www.NavPress.com
or call 1.800.366.7788 in the United States or 1.800.839.4769 in Canada.

ISBN-13: 978-1-57683-534-0

Cover design by studiogearbox.com
Cover image by photos.com
Creative Team: Gabe Filkey s.c.m., Arvid Wallen, Erin Healy, Kathy Mosier, Glynese Northam

This is a work of fiction. The characters, incidents, and dialogues are products of the author's imagination and are not to be construed as real. Any resemblance to actual events or persons, living or dead, is entirely coincidental.

Published in association with the literary agency of Sara A. Fortenberry.

Carlson, Melody.
  Fool's gold : color me consumed / Melody Carlson.
    p. cm. -- (TrueColors ; 6)
  Summary: A daughter of missionaries from Papua New Guinea spends the summer in Los Angeles with her cousin and ends up in debt after getting caught up in the consumerism of wealthy surfer life.
  ISBN 1-57683-534-0
  [1. Credit cards--Fiction. 2. Surfing--Fiction 3. Cousins--Fiction. 4. Missionaries--Fiction. 5. Christian life--Fiction.] I. Title.
  PZ7.C216637Foo 2005
  [Fic]—dc22
                          2005004168

Printed in the United States of America

4 5 6 7 8 9 10 / 13 12 11 10

Other Books by Melody Carlson

Burnt Orange (NavPress)
Pitch Black (NavPress)
Torch Red (NavPress)
Deep Green (NavPress)
Dark Blue (NavPress)
DIARY OF A TEENAGE GIRL series (Multnomah)
DEGREES OF GUILT series (Tyndale)
Crystal Lies (WaterBrook)
Finding Alice (WaterBrook)
Three Days (Baker)

one

MY COUSIN VANESSA THINKS SHOPPING IS A COMPETITIVE SPORT. HONestly, this girl could go for gold if the Olympic committee ever figured out how physically demanding clothes shopping really is. I am so puffed that I think I might die at the mall this afternoon. And I'm a missionary kid (otherwise known as an MK) who can go on a walkabout for kilometers without whinging—well, not much anyway.

But Vanessa is a force to be reckoned with today with her Gucci shoes and plastic Prada purse (loaded with her daddy's plastic cards) as well as her accumulation of brightly colored shopping bags, which she steadily collects until she passes some off to me to lug for her. I finally realize that this girl is not about to give up until she finds the *perfect* T-shirt. And she seems to have something quite specific in mind because I've shown her dozens that I thought were adequate. But she is driven. In fact, she reminds me of that ridiculous bunny rabbit that used to be on telly commercials—the one for the batteries that just keep going and going and going. Vanessa is even wearing pink. Finally I tell my cousin I am wrecked and think I'll grab a lemon squash in the food area until she finishes up.

"A lemon what?" she asks.

"You know, a fizzy drink, lolly water, soda pop, whatever you

Yanks call it. I just need a break is all."

"You're not tired, are you?" Her wide blue eyes look incredulous, almost as if she thinks I have a few kangaroos loose in the top paddock. Although I'm thinking the same thing about her.

I nod. "Yeah, I reckon I am. Do you mind terribly?"

She smiles. "I just love it when you say 'reckon' and 'terribly' and 'fizzy drink.' You sound like such a little Aussie."

As usual, that embarrasses me. Besides, we don't even live in Australia—my parents are missionaries on the island of Papua New Guinea just north of there. "I can't help how I talk, Vanessa," I explain for about the twentieth time. "That's how everyone talks at my school. The accent tends to rub off when all your mates are from Down Under. Trust me, my mum is always correcting my English."

"Well, I think it's adorable, Hannah. But I can't believe you're flaking out on me already. The only reason I brought you along today was because I thought you could use a little—well, you know—help." The way she says the word *help*, you'd think she's offering me a kidney transplant or something. Then she glances at my outfit, taking in my faded logo T-shirt, baggy cargo pants with a hole in one knee, and ancient rubber thongs that were once purple but now look more like the color of old beets. "I mean, those clothes are okay for the jungle or working in the yard. But you don't really want to go around LA looking like, well, like a missionary kid."

I roll my eyes. "That's *like* what I am, Vanessa." I try not to show my pride at picking up this Yankee slang word *like*. It's *like* they use it as a verb and an adverb and just about any other sort of word. It's *like* this and *like* that. And I've *like* been trying to insert it here and there just so I'll fit in better.

"I *know* you're a missionary kid," she continues, "but you don't have to go around advertising it. I mean, unless you want people to feel sorry for you, and you plan to pass the cup around like your parents do when they go to churches to raise their mission money."

Well, I don't let it show, but that last comment stung a bit. Oh, I realize that it probably seems odd to someone like Vanessa that my parents go on furlough every six years to raise support funds. But it's not as if we enjoy this six-month ordeal of tripping about the States begging for money so that my parents can return to the mission field for six more years of hard work and precious little appreciation while I get stuck back in a kids' group home and the mission school. It's not as if we're over here having a great big party. It was a low blow for Vanessa to say that about my parents.

But then I guess she can't help it. She takes after her mum. And it was actually her mum's suggestion that Vanessa take me shopping today. I reckon Aunt Lori's embarrassed to have me seen at their house while my parents are traveling about the States. My dad told me that Aunt Lori was the original "material girl" and that Madonna only came up with that song after meeting her. Of course, he says this with no malice. But it's not exactly a lie either. Well, except for the Madonna part, since I'm fairly sure Aunt Lori has never actually met the pop star. But certainly, no one can deny that Aunt Lori enjoys being rich.

I've also heard that my dad's brother, Uncle Ron, never would've gotten so wealthy without his wife's constant "encouragement." (My mum actually says "nagging" when she doesn't know I'm listening.) Mum also said once that Aunt Lori used to be one of those women with "champagne taste on a beer budget." But it looks like she can have all the champagne she wants now.

To say I was pretty shocked when I saw how drastically things have changed for my relatives is quite an understatement. The last time we were in the States, back when Vanessa and I were about eleven, they still lived in a regular three-bedroom house in a regular neighborhood. Oh, her dad's business was doing well and growing, no doubt about that. But they were by no means wealthy, and Vanessa was just a regular girl back then—not all that different from me. Other than the accent. And the two of us had such an ace time together just doing regular things like riding bikes and watching Disney videos and stuff.

But now it seems that everything's changed. Uncle Ron's custodial business has been wildly successful, and as a result they now live in this enormous house in a very posh neighborhood and have an inground pool, which I've rather enjoyed this past week, as well as all sorts of other amenities. We're talking lifestyles of the rich and famous here. Well, perhaps only rich, since Johnson's Janitorial Services may be well-known but is probably not considered famous—at least not by Hollywood standards. And from what I can see, Hollywood standards seem to rule in my cousin's household. Well, at least with Vanessa and Aunt Lori. Uncle Ron still appears to have both feet planted on terra firma.

"Looks like you'll be pretty comfortable this summer, Hannah," my dad observed when we first arrived at their amazing home last week. "Talk about landing in the lap of luxury."

"Are you sure this is the right address?" My mum peered up at the mustard-colored stucco mansion in front of us.

"This is it," said Dad as he pulled up in our furlough car (an old blue Taurus station wagon with a dent in the right front fender). The circular driveway was lined with pruned shrubs and made entirely of bricks.

"Maybe we shouldn't park our car here," said Mum. "It looks so out of place."

"Do you want me to park it out on the street, Brenda?" My dad's voice was getting slightly irritated.

Mum laughed nervously. "No, I guess not."

Then Dad reached over and patted her hand. "Don't worry about it, honey. They're still just Ron and Lori. And they still put their pants on one leg at a time."

"But their pants probably cost an arm and a leg now."

As it turns out, Mum was close. Because I kid you not, I actually witnessed Vanessa purchasing a pair of jeans that cost nearly $300 today—*$300!* I could not believe it. How can a pair of blue jeans be worth that much?

"Why are they so expensive?" I whispered, not wanting to look like a complete bumpkin, as the sales clerk wrapped the precious blue jeans in lavender-colored tissue paper and then slipped them into a sleek bag with ribbon handles.

"They're Armani." As if that explained everything. "And besides, they're on sale."

Armani. That must be like Gucci and Prada, the other two designer names that I've learned this past week. Now I can only wonder what that pink plastic Prada purse must've set her back. And I happen to think it's pretty ugly.

So as I sit here in the food court, drinking my lemon squash (known as a Sprite here) and people watching, I begin to notice that (a) most of the shoppers are teenage girls or young women; (b) they wear clothes very similar to Vanessa's; (c) for the most part, they carry bags from the same stores that Vanessa has been in; and (d) I most definitely do *not* fit in. In fact, I'm sure I look like someone not only from a different country but probably from an entirely different planet. The funny thing is that all my mates back in PNG dress like I'm dressed, and we were all under the impression that the "grunge look" was still in vogue. But I guess we are behind the times.

After a while I notice this security guard watching me with what I'm sure is suspicion. My guess is that this cop figures I don't belong here either, and he probably thinks I look dodgey, like I'm planning a great heist. So I just smile at him and wave. He quickly looks away, then says something into the walkie-talkie thing pinned to his chest.

Finally Vanessa comes back, looking over the moon, and shows me her "prize." She pulls out a pale blue T-shirt that is so thin you can actually see right through it and says, "I can't believe I found it!"

I touch the flimsy fabric. "But won't your bra show through, Vanessa?"

She laughs. "That's the whole point."

"You want the guys to be perving at your bra?"

"I'll make sure to wear a very cool bra with it, Hannah. Don't get all freaked. That's how it's supposed to be."

I try not to look too stunned, but then I see the price tag and nearly fall off my chair. "You paid $190 for *this*?"

She smiles with what I would describe as a placating smile (the kind you reserve for small children or dimwits), and then she gently slips the shirt back into the bag. "It's a *Prada*. The latest design and the only one left in the store. My friend Elisa is going to be totally jealous."

"Why?"

"Because she wanted one just like it, and now I've gotten the last one."

"I'd think your mate would be totally relieved. You just saved her nearly $200 on a shirt that can't possibly be worth five bucks."

Vanessa laughs. "You just don't get it, Hannah. But wait until you see this top on me with my new jeans. Then you might start to understand fashion."

Just then her cell phone rings, doing its little tinkling musical thing, and suddenly Vanessa is chatting away with one of her mates—Elisa Rodriguez, it turns out—going on and on about how she "searched absolutely everywhere" until she finally found the "perfect Prada T-shirt" and how "hot" she's going to look in it at the party tomorrow night. Yeah, yeah.

I walk over to the bin and dump my paper cup, pausing to look at that cop who is still eyeing me. Once again, I smile and wave at him, and to my surprise, he actually smiles back this time. I want to walk over, say hello, and ask him what he thinks about all these silly girls spending thousands—no, make that millions and probably billions—of dollars on strange names like Prada and Gucci and Armani. Does he, like me, think it is perfectly ridiculous? Probably not since this overpriced, designer-driven mall is paying his salary. Alright, sometimes I wonder if there's something wrong with me. Why don't I get it? Will I ever really fit in here?

So as I sit here half-listening to Vanessa earbashing Elisa, I start to daydream. I remember this old fairy tale called *The Emperor's New Clothes* that I had enjoyed as a child. Only, in my mind, I now change it to *The Empress' New Clothes*, starring Vanessa Johnson. In my version, my cousin insists that she will wear only the best and most expensive garments in the design industry. "That does not cost enough!" she screams at one of the lesser designers. Finally a designer comes up and says that his outfit will cost one million dollars and will be the most expensive clothing ever made. (Okay, maybe one million is too cheap.) So Empress Vanessa waits for a week and the designer returns with his amazing outfit. But when he opens the gold-plated box with layers of tissue, it is empty. "Where are my clothes?" demands Vanessa. He smiles and says, "Right here, Empress. But you must understand that I have used the finest fibers known to mankind. The threads are so delicate that only those who truly know and appreciate exquisite design can see them." Then, of course, Vanessa nods, pretending she can see the nonexistent clothing. "Go ahead," she tells him. "Help me put them on." And after Vanessa dons her million-dollar outfit, she parades all over Beverly Hills in nothing but her underwear, and everyone who sees her simply laughs and—

"*Hannah?*"

I look up to see Vanessa standing over me, looking impatient and perhaps a bit weary, although fully clothed. "What?" I ask sleepily.

"I *said*, are you ready to go home?"

The next thing I know, we are driving down the road, and despite all my criticisms of my cousin's lavish lifestyle and expensive taste, I find that I'm enjoying her Yank tank, which is actually this gorgeous silver convertible. It's a Ford Thunderbird that she says is "retro," whatever that's supposed to mean. But I reckon it's the most luxurious car I've ever been in. I'm leaning back into the soft leather seat as the breeze tosses my hair, and for a brief moment I imagine what it might feel like to be rich and carefree like my cousin.

But then I look down and notice the hole in the knee of my worn-out cargo pants, and I realize that I am still just Hannah Johnson, the MK misfit from the other side of the world. And, I admit, I think I am feeling just the slightest bit jealous.

two

VANESSA MAY HAVE HER FAULTS, BUT STINGINESS IS NOT ONE OF THEM. On our shopping trip she tried to get me to buy things with her dad's credit card. And I was actually tempted by a pair of jeans, until I saw the price tag. Then I knew I couldn't in good conscience spend my hardworking uncle's cash so frivolously. And so I declined. But when we get back to Vanessa's house, I almost wish I'd bought them.

"So what did you get, Hannah?" asks Aunt Lori as soon as we're inside. I'm helping Vanessa carry her bags, and I reckon my aunt assumes that some of these purchases are mine.

"I didn't see anything I couldn't live without." I set the bags on the end of the enormous granite brek-kie bar.

"I couldn't talk her into anything," says Vanessa as she piles her purse and bags alongside the others.

Aunt Lori frowns. "What are we going to do with you, Hannah?"

I look out the big bay window, longing to escape this conversation by plunging myself into the cool depths of that beautiful pool. Instead, I turn to my aunt and say, "I don't know, what would you like to do with me?"

This makes her laugh. Then she reaches over and playfully tugs a strand of my long hair. "Well, if you weren't so tall and thin, I'd make you borrow some clothes from Vanessa or even me." Then she seems to study me. "You're an attractive girl, Hannah, but you really need some fashion direction. If you want to survive a summer with Vanessa and her friends, that is." She glances over at Vanessa, who is frowning. "Don't you think?"

Vanessa redirects her attention to the contents of her bags and says, "Yeah, I guess."

I'm feeling really uncomfortable now, as if I'm this huge intrusion into their lives. "I, uh, I don't have to spend *all* my time with Vanessa and her mates," I say quickly. "I was actually thinking I might look for a job or something."

"Someone looking for a job?" calls a male voice from down the hallway that leads to the four-car garage.

"Hi, Ron," says Aunt Lori as he pecks her on the cheek.

"Hello, ladies." Then he focuses his attention on me. "Seriously, Hannah, did I hear you say you were looking for a job?"

I nod. "It wouldn't hurt to earn some money for uni."

"Uni?" He looks at me as if I'm speaking a foreign language.

"You know, university. What do you call it?"

"Oh, right. University or college."

"Right." But I'm thinking, *Isn't that what I just said?*

"Well, if you're serious about working, I just might have something for you, Hannah."

Suddenly I envision myself dressed as a cleaner, scrubbing floors and picking up rubbish in some stuffy old office building. But maybe it wouldn't be so bad. At least I'd earn some cash and have something to do besides shadowing my cousin. "I'm rather good with a mop," I tell him. "We all have to do our fair share at the group home on base. I certainly know how to scrub toilets, and I even do windows."

He laughs. "I wasn't actually thinking of a janitorial job for you, but I do like your spirit."

"What, then?"

"Oh, Hannah," interrupts Vanessa, "you don't want to waste your whole summer working for Dad when you could be having fun."

"That's true," says Uncle Ron. "You could be out having fun with Vanessa. I don't want to cramp your—"

"No worries," I say quickly. "I'd absolutely *love* a job, even if it was only cleaning and whatnot."

He nods. "Okay, then, are you good on a computer?"

"I could give it a go." I'm actually quite competent, but I don't like to brag.

"And I know you're good with people."

"I reckon."

"And your accent would be charming on the phone."

"So what's the deal?" I ask eagerly.

"One of my receptionists didn't show today. I heard she was going to Las Vegas for the weekend. But she didn't bother to tell anyone she was taking the day off. And it's not the first time she's pulled this, either."

"So she's getting the sack?"

He nods. "You want to give it a try, Hannah?"

"If you reckon I can handle it."

He grins. "I *reckon* you can. That is, if you can handle the hours. Are you much of a morning person?"

I look at my watch. It has two faces—one set on Yank time and one still set for PNG. "Well, it's about three a.m. in New Guinea right now. That's pretty early and I'm still awake."

"Good point. Your hours will be six in the morning until two in the afternoon."

"Ugh," calls Vanessa from the other side of the room where she's showing today's purchases to her mum. "That sounds like pure torture to me."

"It'll be alright," I assure her. "And getting off at two in the afternoon still leaves time to muck around."

Uncle Ron nods. "And Vanessa will barely be up by then anyway."

"Yeah, sure, Dad."

"Can you start on Monday, Hannah?"

"No worries!" So we shake on it, and it's settled.

"You can use my Jeep to get to work," he offers. "That is, if you have a driver's license. Do you?"

I nod. "I got one when my dad did, just last week. I did even better on the test than he did, but don't tell him I told."

"Great. Do you think you can manage driving on the right side of the road? Or maybe I should let you practice this weekend. The keys are in the console of the Jeep if you want to take it out for a spin. Just remember to take my golf clubs out of the back before you go. And pop out the CD player when you park it; there's a locking case under the seat for it."

"Why's that?"

"It's the first thing that'll get stolen downtown. I had a soft top slit open when I forgot to remove it once. Unfortunately it costs more to replace the soft top than the CD player."

"Okay, I'll remember that. Thanks, Uncle Ron. That's really cool of you." And then I can't help myself. I throw my arms around him and give him a big hug. "I really appreciate it."

"In fact, just go ahead and consider the Jeep your vehicle while you're here with us, Hannah. I rarely use it anyway. I've considered getting rid of it, but it's handy for my clubs."

"As if you ever play golf anymore," says Aunt Lori as she joins us. "Your uncle thinks that life begins and ends with work." Now she turns and looks at me more closely, but she has this funny expression on her face, as if she's deliberating over something. "Well, Hannah," she says slowly, "now that you've got a job, you might *have* to rethink your wardrobe. She can't go into the office wearing pants with holes in them, now can she, Ron?"

He just shrugs as he heads for the fridge. "I'm sure you girls can work out those little details." He takes out a stubby and pops off the lid. I admit I was a bit surprised when I first saw that Uncle Ron drinks beer. I'm not even sure why, except that alcohol is forbidden on the mission (although I have mates who break this rule). But Uncle Ron usually has only one or two before dinner. I've never seen him slaughtered or tanked or anything disrespectful. I think it's just his way of chilling out after a long day.

Aunt Lori nods victoriously. "Yes, I'm sure that we can. Can't we, Hannah?"

And so it seems my fate is sealed. I promise my aunt that I'll go shopping with her tomorrow. "Just a few things." I look back at the pool to hide my nervousness. "And, please, not the shopping center where Vanessa took me today."

"Why not?" asks Vanessa. She is flopped down on their enormous, oversized leather sectional, absently flipping through the millions of channels they receive on their flat-screen plasma telly that takes up half the wall.

"Because I don't need fancy designer clothes. I just need something suitable for work."

Aunt Lori pats my back. "Don't worry, Hannah. You'll be in good hands with me."

Vanessa just laughs. "Yeah, right, Mom. You have okay taste for an old lady, but you're totally clueless when it comes to—"

"An *old* lady?" Thankfully, Aunt Lori is now distracted from me as she emphatically defends her youth to her seventeen-year-old daughter.

"Anyone mind if I take a dip in the pool?" I ask, not wishing to get caught in a fight over whether Aunt Lori is really an old bag or not.

"Nice to see *someone's* using the pool," calls Uncle Ron as he heads off to his office. He spends most of his spare time in there. I'm not sure if he's actually working or just escaping the bickering between his wife and daughter. And since I've witnessed how they can really get into it over practically nothing, I just want to rack off sometimes too. Like now. It's not that I don't understand. I reckon my mum and I have had our fair share of fights, but not living with your parents can spare you a lot of arguing.

I go upstairs to the guest room that I'm using this summer. They gave me my pick, and I chose the smallest one because it felt cozier, plus it has a view of the pool. And although it is the smallest, it's about twice as big as the dorm room I have back home, which I share with three other girls! In addition to that, it also has its own "bathroom" that not only has a bath and shower, but the dunny and sink are actually in there too. So American!

I tug on my still-damp bathers that I forgot to hang up after my morning swim. And once again, I'm caught off guard by the large mirrors on the closet doors. I'm unaccustomed to seeing my whole self like this. And so I just stand there a moment and stare—and after feeling like such a misfit at the shops today, I take a sort of physical inventory of myself.

Aunt Lori's right—I am quite tall at five foot ten (U.S. measurements—see, I'm already making the leap away from metrics. Oh, my primary school math teacher would be so proud!). That makes me nearly six inches taller than Vanessa. And although I'm thin, I'm not nearly as skinny as I used to be. In fact, I was quite relieved when I finally got breasts last year. I honestly thought I might never get any. Even Sophie (my best mate in PNG) was worried for me. So at least I have a bit of a figure now, even if I'm not the hottest chick around. And I am nicely tanned. Both my cousin and aunt were impressed with that. Despite worries about cancer, tanned skin is still desirable here in the States, although I've heard that some people get it spray painted on or go into some kind of a booth with light bulbs, which I do find rather curious. Not that I can help being tanned, coming from a place where it's constantly like summertime.

Vanessa and I used to have the same color hair—my mum called it honey blonde. But as I got older, my hair got darker. And although it lightens with the sun—especially on the ends, which nearly reach my midback—my hair is more of a dusty brown color than anything else. Rather boring, actually. But Vanessa confessed that she gets hers professionally highlighted, so she looks more like a blonde than ever. I have to admit it looks quite nice on her and fairly natural too. But then, she has blue eyes, whereas I have green. So perhaps I'm destined to have boring brown hair.

Finally I tell myself that I am who I am, take it or leave it, and that standing here in my damp bathers (which, as Vanessa was quick to point out, have seen better days considering the spot on my bum that has worn rather thin) and obsessing about my appearance is not going to change a thing. So I grab a big, thick towel, wrap it around myself, slip on my rubber thongs, and hurry downstairs. Vanessa is absorbed in one of those reality shows that I frankly find either terribly boring or completely disgusting. In fact, I already told her that if she wants to see people eating grubs, she should come to New Guinea. It's no big deal there.

The big fancy kitchen, which I've discovered gets little use for actual cooking, is, as usual, vacant. I'm not sure where Aunt Lori is, but I know that she doesn't even think about tea (or what they call dinner) until nearly seven, and often she just orders take-away. But I have been trying to help out as much as possible. And I think my aunt appreciates it, since Vanessa is quite an expert at slacking.

I go outside where the temperature is about twenty degrees hotter than the air-conditioned house. Feeling chilled from my damp bathers, I find a lounge chair that's been baking in the sun and slowly lower myself down onto it, taking a sharp breath as my body sinks into the heat.

And there I lie until my skin begins to feel hot and prickly. The heat in Southern California is different than in New Guinea due to the humidity. Apparently Los Angeles was created on an arid desert. Water gets pumped here through aqueducts from hundreds of miles away. So although there is green grass and foliage and trees, the air remains quite dry. In PNG, everything is saturated with moisture. You can't leave a pair of damp canvas shoes in the closet for more than a day before spectacular forms of mold take over. That's why rubber thongs are so popular. And dry foods will go bad if they're not properly stored in airtight containers. Even tinned food can rust. It's just very, very moist, even during the dry season.

During the wet season, it rains every day at about the same time in the afternoon. But I actually love those rains. To me they are a cleansing, cooling time. And when the sun comes out, the world looks washed and new and ready to go on. My dad says it rains in Southern California too and that it can even flood here, but I think that must be quite rare. I don't recall having seen it for myself.

Finally it feels as if my skin is actually sizzling. Even my bathers are dry as a biscuit now. Feeling thirsty and hot, I tiptoe across the sun-baked deck, then climb onto the diving board and stare down at the crystal-clear water below me. This immaculate pool with its tiled deck is maintained by a pool guy who never wears a shirt but apparently knows his business because, as usual, it shimmers like polished turquoise. Perfection.

After a couple of tentative bounces on the springy board, I go up into the air and plunge into the water, splattering its perfect surface with a rather sloppy dive, I'm afraid. And as I swim beneath the cool layers of water, I think that perhaps this will be a great summer after all.

When I finally come up for air, I notice that Vanessa has decided to join me for a swim. Only she's not alone. I don't know the girl who's arranging a spot on a lounge chair with her, but I suspect it might be Elisa Rodriguez, since her hair is shiny black and she appears to be Hispanic—and beautiful. But what really gets my attention is how both of these girls look absolutely fabulous in their tiny bathers (bikinis, actually) and oversized sunnies (which Yanks call sunglasses or shades or dark-glasses—I'm never sure of the correct lingo) and brightly colored sandals, which probably cost a week's worth of my soon-to-be wages. Or more.

Honestly, everything about these girls looks unbelievably expensive—their hair, their teeth, their tans, their jewelry. It probably adds up to thousands, and they're not even dressed! They both look incredibly perfect, like something you see on the telly or in a slick magazine. And I am reminded once again of how I really don't fit in around here at all. I'm like a reffo, and I'm afraid it's going to be a very long summer.

three

I WAKE UP VERY EARLY THE FOLLOWING MORNING. AFTER TWO WEEKS, I
think I'm still on PNG time. But realizing that I'll be getting up early
next week for my new job anyway, I decide to just "surf the lag," as
my dad likes to say. He never gets concerned about jet lag. He says
if he's awake, he might as well enjoy being awake—using the quiet
time to pray or read. And if he's sleepy, he tries to slip in a nap when
no one is looking. "No worries."

So it is that I decide to surf the lag myself. I tiptoe downstairs at
five a.m. and search about the bookshelves until I find a paperback,
which happens to be an adventure story about sharks (or after darks,
as we sometimes call them). I suspect this book must belong to my
uncle because I'm sure, after reading the sensational back cover, that
it's too gory for either Vanessa or Aunt Lori. But it appeals to me. So
I sit down and read. Before long I've read several chapters, and the
story is quite enthralling, which is why I nearly jump out of my skin
when I hear Uncle Ron saying, "Good morning."

"Oh!" I take a recovery breath as I close the book and look up
at him.

He nods to the paperback and laughs. "Pretty scary stuff,
huh?"

"I reckon. Have you read it?"

"Yes. I didn't want to go anywhere near the ocean for several weeks after."

"I know what you mean."

"Want some coffee? Or maybe that Aussie influence turned you into a tea drinker?"

"I like both, actually. Most of my mates only drink tea. But we had a Yankee couple as house parents a couple years back. Alex and Callie were newlyweds from Seattle, Washington."

"Coffee capital of the universe."

"That's what they told us. And they had packages of Starbucks beans shipped every month. By the time their one-year stint was up, a couple of us had become regular coffee addicts."

He laughs as he heads into the kitchen.

"Fortunately, they left their coffee machine behind, and the grinder too, although the grinder broke down last year."

"You should take another one back with you. We might even have a spare we don't need."

I set the book aside and follow him, noticing how much he looks like my dad from the back. They have the same shuffling way of walking. Seeing that makes me miss my parents. "Were you and Dad close when you were younger?" I ask as I perch myself on one of the comfortable padded stools at the brek-kie bar.

"Well, Rick is five years older, you know, and when we were growing up, it seemed like a fairly wide gap to me. But I always looked up to him. I guess I admired your dad a lot."

"What did you think when he decided to become a missionary?"

"At first I was pretty surprised." He pushes the button on their coffeemaker and waits for the loud grinding of the beans to finish. Then he turns back to me. "Oh, I knew that Rick took his religion very seriously, but I just didn't think he'd take it *that* far. But I was in high school by then, and I was into sports and girls and partying and—" he stops himself, embarrassed, I think. "Well, you know how it goes, Hannah." Then he frowns. "Or maybe you don't."

I laugh. "Actually, I do. I reckon most people assume that MKs are just like their parents. But let me tell you, it's not always like that. Some of the kids back on base go ga-ga as soon as they hit high school."

"What do they do that's so *ga-ga*?" He leans forward with interest.

"Well, they smoke their cancer sticks and drink their beer. Some even get into drugs."

"Where do missionary kids get drugs?"

I shrug. "Where does anyone get drugs?"

"Yeah, I guess you're right." Then he frowns slightly. "But you're not into any of that, are you?"

"No way. I think drugs are absolutely crazy. Why would you want to mess with your mind like that? I happen to think God gave me a pretty good mind without mucking it up with some weird chemicals."

"How about your brothers? Did they ever do any wild things? They seem like such responsible young men."

"Well, you probably never heard about how Mark went slightly bonkers during his first year of college. His grades were so far up the creek that I don't know how he kept from getting suspended. But then he got off his bum, and he even made the dean's list this year."

"That's great."

"My parents were pretty relieved."

"And I heard your brothers are both taking summer classes."

"Yeah, Dad and Mum plan to visit them when they're in Dallas next month. I'm trying not to be too jealous, but if I earn enough money, maybe I'll be able to fly out there in the fall. Matthew is certain that I should go to school there too."

Uncle Ron laughs. "The responsible big brother. He reminds me a lot of your dad."

"Yeah, Matt's almost too good to believe sometimes. Although I really do love him."

"I think a lot of firstborn kids are like that." Uncle Ron turns back to the cupboard and removes two very large, brightly colored coffee mugs. Sometimes it seems that everything in Southern California is like that—big and bright and slightly overdone. But it's kind of fun.

"I reckon. My best mate, Sophie, is like that, and she's a firstborn too. I sometimes think Sophie's the main reason I haven't gotten into trouble yet."

"Yet?" He turns and hands me a cup of steaming coffee.

I laugh. "No worries, Uncle Ron. I'm not really planning anything."

He pretends to be greatly relieved as he holds up a carton of something. "Cream?"

"Huh?" It takes me a moment. "Oh, yeah, white, please. And I take a bit of sugar too."

He brings the carton of cream and the sugar dispenser over to me, and I adjust my coffee and take a sip. "Delicious," I say. "Thanks."

"As good as the coffee in New Guinea?" he asks in a teasing tone. "Your dad is always bragging about it, and he sends us some at Christmas, but between you and me, we're not that fond of it. Or maybe something happens in the shipping."

I sip the scalding java and smile. "I think this coffee is better than what we drink at home. To be honest, the stuff we drink is pretty gross. It comes in a big can and I don't think it's even from New Guinea. Sophie says it's probably recycled grounds from some little old ladies' missionary society—you know, like the ones who send us their secondhand tea bags."

"Does that stuff really happen?"

"I don't know for sure. It may be an urban legend. Or would that be a global legend? I did a paper on urban legends last year. It was a crackup!"

"Tell me one."

So I tell him the one about a guy named Fred Gay who was supposedly a Qantas employee flying on a free pass. "So Fred goes to his assigned seat but another guy is sitting there, so Fred thinks *no worries* and just goes and finds himself another seat. Then an air hostess goes up to the guy in Fred's seat and asks, 'Are you Gay?' Well, the man gets quite embarrassed, then nods. And so she tells him he'll have to leave. Just as the poor man is reaching for his bag, Fred Gay stands up and shows her his pass and says, 'I'm Gay.' So then she tells him that he'll have to leave. But now a bloke on the other side of the aisle is going schiz at her. He stands up and yells, 'Well, I'm gay too, and so is my partner. Does that mean we all have to leave?'"

My uncle cracks up laughing and then looks at his watch. "Well, I better head into the office now."

"You work on Saturdays?"

He nods. "No rest for the wicked."

I frown. "You're not wicked, Uncle Ron."

"Depends on who you're talking to, Hannah." As he leaves, I wonder if he means my parents. Not that they preach at him exactly, but I know they're concerned about the "spiritual condition" of Ron,

Lori, and Vanessa. And I know that they pray for this family on a regular basis. I'm supposed to pray for them too, but the truth is, I forget most of the time. In fact, I haven't been praying about much of anything lately. It's not that I quit believing in God. I still do. But I guess I'm just tired of everything. Sophie questioned me about this as I was getting ready to go on furlough.

"You forgot your Bible," she said, holding up the well-worn leather Bible that my parents got me when I was twelve.

"I'm traveling light," I told her, which was true. I was taking only one very light port for a checked bag and then my pack.

"But it's your *Bible*," she said emphatically, as if informing me that it was the oxygen mask that could save my life while flying across the Pacific.

"Truly?"

"Hannah." A shocked expression took over her face. "You can't go to the States without your Bible. It's your sword and your light and your compass and your—well, you know what it is, and you'll be lost without it."

I zipped my backpack shut and, tossing a strap over my shoulder, stood up. "Well, I'm into minimalism," I told her. "Trying to get by without much, you know."

She shook her head. "But not without your Bible."

"Don't stress, Sophie. I'll be alright. Do you really think God's gonna turn his back on me just because I'm not packing a Bible?"

"That's not it. My worry is that you might turn your back on him."

"Oh, Sophie." I gave her my best exasperated expression. But then I heard my dad calling, asking me if I was ready to roll. So I hugged my best friend and told her I'd e-mail her as soon as I got settled. "Catchya!"

"I'll be praying for you," she told me with a troubled brow.

And I have no doubts that she is praying for me. But I haven't even e-mailed her yet. I'm not sure why because I really do love Sophie, and I miss her a lot. But something in me wants to take a break right now. My whole life has been nothing but mission schools, church, and totally "God-centered" activities. I'm not complaining. Well, maybe I am. Maybe I'm just tired of being a missionary kid, living in the spiritual shadow of my parents. Maybe I'm not even sure about what I personally believe anymore. Or perhaps I'm taking a spiritual furlough of sorts. I'm not sure what's going on with me, but I reckon I don't really want to think about it either. And the truth is, I haven't really missed my Bible yet. I do feel a bit guilty about that, probably out of habit, but I'm telling myself that it's going to be perfectly fine. I'm telling myself that God is bigger than this, bigger than me, and he must understand what I'm going through—since he's God and all. And in the end, I'm sure that I'll come out on top.

"Goodness, you're up early," says Aunt Lori when she comes into the kitchen looking bleary-eyed and barely awake.

"It's nearly nine o'clock."

"I know. But Vanessa never gets up this early."

"Well, my internal clock is still a little mucked up." I nod toward the coffeemaker. "Uncle Ron made coffee."

"Good for him." She heads straight for the pot. "If I could just remember to set it up the night before, no one would have to bother in the morning." She pours herself a cup and takes a sip. "I guess I should put that on Consuela's list."

Consuela is their housekeeper. She's about sixty or seventy, I think, and drives a tinny little car that looks like it's going to die at any moment. She comes in every weekday for several hours and always looks hot and worn-out even before she starts working. But, seriously, that woman can clean. I watched her one day, without her knowing it, and she just gets in there and goes for it. I wanted to tell her she should slow down a bit. She could make more money since she gets paid by the hour, but she barely speaks English, and I suspect my aunt wouldn't be pleased with that suggestion anyway.

"Maybe I could make the coffee for you in the mornings," I offer. "I want to help out around here, you know. And if there are things that need doing, I hope you'll feel free to—"

"We're not going to turn you into our personal slave, Hannah." She opens the fridge and takes out the orange juice. "This summer is supposed to be fun for you." She pours a large glassful. "Want some?"

"Sure." She hands me the glass and goes back for another. Now this is another thing that amazes me about Southern California. They drink orange juice by the gallon here. Oh, we have it in New Guinea sometimes, but even then we only drink small *juice* glassfuls. To drink a huge glass would be considered extravagant or wasteful. But not here. Extravagance seems to be the rule. Just watch a few ads on the telly and you know this is true. They're filled with slogans like "You're worth it" and "Not more than you need . . . just more than you're used to." Everything in this country is about excess. Like the show where Paris Hilton and Nicole Richie go "roughing it" at some farm, when both those girls are actually millionaires and used to having everything handed to them on a silver platter. The other thing that I find unbelievable is this constant attention to appearances and fashion. Vanessa is addicted to these "reality" shows where they take some poor overweight and not terribly attractive girl and totally transform her with plastic surgery, dentistry, weight trainers, fashion experts, the works. By the time they're done, she doesn't even look like the same person.

At first I was somewhat shocked and disgusted by all this, but I reckon I'm getting used to it now.

"I'm already disappointed that Ron has talked you into working for him," my aunt continues as she sits down with her juice and flips through a thick fashion magazine. "I wanted you to have a fun and carefree summer with Vanessa. You know, the way you girls used to."

I sigh. "Well, we were a lot younger then. We liked things like bikes and Barbie dolls and painting our toenails purple."

She laughs. "Vanessa still does purple toenails occasionally. The only difference now is that someone else usually does the painting."

"Really?" Now, I'm not even sure why this should surprise me, but it does. "Vanessa has someone to paint her toenails?"

"Lan is our favorite. She's Vietnamese and does the most magnificent manicures and pedicures." Aunt Lori examines a shiny, pale nail with a white tip that looks like pure perfection to me, especially compared to my stubby nails, which might possibly be dirty as well. I tuck them into my lap just in case.

"In fact," my aunt continues, "I should probably schedule an appointment with Lan for next week." Then she looks back at me. "And speaking of appointments, I wanted to take you shopping for work clothes today, but I completely forgot that I have a luncheon date at the club. And, well, that doesn't leave much time for—"

"It's okay." I hope I don't appear too relieved. "Maybe I could just—"

"Vanessa could take you. Oh, I know she overwhelmed you a bit yesterday, Hannah. But that's only because you're coming from such a different culture. Your mom told me that you'd probably experience a little culture shock. I guess it's not easy adjusting to American life."

I nod. "Yeah, it's been kind of challenging. But you guys are great," I say quickly. "And I love being in your new home, and the pool is fantastic."

She smiles. "Oh, I'm so glad you like it."

"But as far as shopping, maybe I'll just head out on my own. Uncle Ron thought I should practice driving. And I remember seeing some shops just a few kilometers, I mean miles, from here—"

"Oh, you don't mean Stanley Square, do you?"

"Well, they had what appeared to be a clothes shop. I think it was called Ross something."

She frowned. "That's Ross Dress for Less."

I smiled. "For less? Meaning the prices are lower?"

"Oh, Hannah, you must learn that you get what you pay for."

I consider Vanessa's spiderweb-thin T-shirt that cost nearly $200 and just nod dumbly. "But it's only for work, Aunt Lori. I shouldn't spend a fortune on work clothes, should I?" I don't admit to her that I am already feeling a bit pov or that my summer allowance that Dad gave me right before he left only a week ago has dwindled down to less than two hundred dollars already, which is another reason I will be glad to have a job. I had no idea it would be so expensive to do "nothing" with Vanessa. But then, I haven't wanted her to pay for everything for me either. Although she usually offers. She is quite generous with her dad's money.

Aunt Lori sighs and looks as if she's making an unforgivable social faux pas. "Well, I guess it won't hurt for you to get a few items at *Ross Dress for Less.*" She acts like I've suggested we shop at the Salvation Army or Goodwill. Not that I haven't shopped in those places before. Last time we were here, Mum and I found some awesome prices on terrific duds. We shipped two boxes back home, and it was like Christmas when we opened them. In fact, I wonder if there are any of those stores in this neighborhood. Probably not. And I'm afraid if I was spotted at one, I would probably scandalize poor Aunt Lori and Vanessa to no end.

"Thanks," I tell her, feeling like I have just won a tremendous victory in the world of Yankee fashion.

"But why don't you take Vanessa along with you. She might be able to help you find some, well, some more *appropriate* things."

"She's welcome to come if she wants. But she might not enjoy it very much. I don't think Ross is exactly her sort of shop."

Aunt Lori laughs. "Well, it might be good for her. Make her appreciate how far we've come during the past five years."

"Yeah." I glance out to the shimmering blue pool that seems to beckon to me like an old friend. "I think I'll go for a swim before I go."

"Good for you. And really, I'm sorry that I have to bail on you for shopping. You have to promise to let me take you another time." She brightens. "Maybe tomorrow. Hey, maybe you and Vanessa and I could go together—just the girls. It would be such fun."

I smile and nod, pretending that such an outing would be absolutely riveting. But the whole idea has me seriously freaked (as Vanessa would say). Three back-to-back days of shopping! I don't know if I can survive this. It's almost bad enough to make me want to pray. Alright, not quite. Besides, I reckon God's got more pressing issues than to rescue someone like me from the tortures of shopping, especially since I'm down here languishing in the lifestyles of the rich and famous while other people are struggling just to get by.

four

"Mom says I'm supposed to go to Ross Dress for Less with you," says Vanessa in a less-than-thrilled voice.

"You don't have to," I tell her. "I'm good on my own. And I don't think a shop like Ross is your kinda thing."

She sighs and looks relieved.

"And really, Vanessa, I don't expect you to feel responsible for me while I'm here. I understand that you have a life and friends and all that. Honestly, I don't want to get in the way. I'm normally quite independent."

"Yeah, I know you are. But I really do like being with you, Hannah. I'm hoping, *actually*, that your Aussie accent will start rubbing off on me. You *reckon* it will?"

I laugh at her poor imitation but assure her there's hope.

"And on second thought," she says, "it might be amusing to see how you do at Ross Dress for Less. Besides that, I could probably help you from making any serious fashion mistakes." Now she's looking unexpectedly enthusiastic. "Hey, it could be like *What Not to Wear*. I could follow you around like the fashion police, and if I catch you getting something totally lame, I could stop you."

Now, the idea of my cousin on my back while I'm trying to find a work outfit is a bit unsettling. "You certain you want to come along? I don't reckon it'll be any fun for you." And then I think of something. "And what if one of your mates saw you at that store? Wouldn't you—"

"Yeah, right!" says Vanessa. "*No worries.* None of my *mates* would be caught dead in a store that pathetic."

"That certainly makes me feel good."

"Oh, I'm not trying to put you down, Hannah. And like you said, you're only getting work clothes. Mom told me that the three of us will go to a good mall tomorrow—to get you some *real* clothes."

Real clothes? Like that see-through Prada number Vanessa picked up yesterday? A top like that would wipe out my entire summer allowance.

It takes Vanessa about an hour to get ready to go. I'm not sure why she goes to so much trouble, especially since she doesn't expect to see anyone she knows at Ross. But maybe she just can't help herself.

"Ready to bail?" I ask when she finally makes an appearance, looking, as usual, perfect.

"Bail on who?"

"You know, *bail*, as in *leave*. Are you ready?"

"Sure." She grins. "Let's bail."

"Do you mind if I drive your dad's Jeep?" I ask as I look somewhat longingly at her gorgeous car.

"I guess not."

"I sort of need practice driving down the wrong side of the road."

"You mean the *right* side."

"*Wrong* side," I protest. "At least where I come from." Then, like a total dag, I open the passenger side of the Jeep and start to climb in.

"Wrong side," points out Vanessa as she waits for me to get out of the way.

"Just getting the keys," I say with what I hope sounds like nonchalance as I reach into the glove box to find them. "I gotta take your dad's golf clubs out of the boot, remember?"

So she gets in and checks her perfect self in the mirror as I lug out the big bag of clubs and set them off in a corner of the garage. Then I come back and get into the right (which feels wrong) side of the Jeep and sit there for a moment to check out the controls and things.

"Can you drive a stick?" she asks.

"You mean manual?"

"Yeah, whatever."

"That's all I've ever driven. The problem is, this is on the wrong side."

"Right side," she corrects me. "See, you use your right hand to shift."

"How do I get the garage door open?" I've seen them do this from their cars, but I've never quite figured it out.

"That button on the visor." She points.

So I push it, and presto, it works. Then I start the Jeep, and only grinding the gears a bit, I begin to roll in reverse until I'm in the driveway. Then, grinding the gears just slightly again, I put it in first, and we move forward.

"Don't you want to close the door?"

I pause and glance at the gaping garage door. "Same button?"

"That's right."

"I hope you know that I'm feeling like a real loser right now," I admit as I slowly back out into the street. "Maybe you'll come visit me someday, and I'll make you sit in the wrong side of the car and drive down the wrong side of the road and see how you like it."

"See," says Vanessa, "you admit it. You guys do drive on the wrong side."

I laugh and realize it's useless to argue.

"Watch out!" she yells as I make a left-hand turn and suddenly find myself on the wrong side of the street. I mean the wrong side for real, and there is a car coming straight at us. I whip the wheel, popping us into the other lane, and just barely miss smacking into a gorgeous black Jaguar. The balding middle-aged man behind the wheel yells a bad word, then gives me the middle-finger salute.

"Wow, that could've been quite a bungle," I say calmly, trying hard to regain some composure, assuming I had any to start with.

Vanessa is just laughing hysterically now, and it's hard not to join in, but I'm focusing on the center line, trying to remember to stay on the "right" side of it, as well as watch for traffic signals and remember which way the little shopping mall is from here. It's all quite unsettling, and embarrassment makes me wish that my cousin had stayed home.

"Turn here," she shouts through giggles when I'm nearly in the intersection.

"Which way?"

"Right!"

And I actually start to turn left.

"The *other* right!" She points to the right and I quickly readjust, screaming the tires around the corner as I attempt to shift down.

I grimace and consider pulling over and asking Vanessa to drive.

"You're a real wild woman!" says Vanessa. I'm not sure, but I think she's actually impressed.

"I didn't mean to do that."

"Okay, it's about a mile down this street, and then it's on the right. The *other* right."

That makes me laugh, and I start to loosen up as I check the speedometer and remind myself that it's miles, not kilometers, so I'm actually going faster than it seems. Whatever the case, I don't want to get a speeding ticket, and I don't want to have a crash. I am wound tighter than a spool by the time we reach the shopping mall.

"That wasn't so bad," says Vanessa, but I know she's just being kind.

"Thanks," I tell her. "I reckon there's room for improvement."

She looks at the storefront now and frowns as if she may be regretting her decision, but I just head for the entrance, pushing open a big glass door and pausing in front of a long line of plastic shopping trolleys.

"Am I supposed to take one of these?"

She shrugs. "Whatever."

So I tentatively remove a bright blue trolley from the end. I'm not even sure why I am doing this. I reckon it's because the portly lady ahead of me did it. One of the wheels on my trolley seems to be sticking and, consequently, having convulsions as I push it toward a table that's loaded with men's wallets and things, going *bluppity-blup, bluppity-blup*. I look at the sea of clothing and merchandise and wonder where I should begin. I decide to head for the nearest rack and make an attempt to look like I know what I'm doing.

Vanessa moans behind me, and I turn around to see that her face is growing a bit pale, as if she's about to chuck up. "What's wrong?" I ask.

She glances over to where three girls about our age stand looking at a rack of clothes, then quickly turns her back to them as she slips on her sunnies. "I *know* those girls," she whispers in a desperate tone.

"But I thought you said none of your mates—"

"They're not my *mates*," she hisses. "They're girls I used to hang with, before we moved, you know. They still go to my old school and—"

"Why don't you say hello to them?"

"No way."

"Why?"

But she doesn't answer; she just turns away and looks toward the door.

"What do you want me to do?" I ask.

"Nothing. I think I'll split for a while. I saw a coffee kiosk down on the other end of the parking lot. Do you mind if I go get a mocha frappé?"

"Of course not." Actually I'm hugely relieved. "Go ahead. And take your time."

"Want me to bring you back a frappé—you know, after a while?"

"Sure, that sounds great."

So just like that, Vanessa is gone, and I am free to figure out this maze of a clothing store on my own. I quickly discover that not everything here is a bargain. The racks in the front are "designer" clothes. Not Prada or Gucci or Armani, but names like Ralph Lauren and Tommy Hilfiger and Liz Claiborne. And although I find their marked-down prices to be a little steep for my budget, I suspect that people like Aunt Lori and Vanessa would think these clothes were cheap and unimpressive. Although I must admit that I do like some of the Hilfiger pieces, and I vaguely recall Sophie bragging to me that her favorite hooded sweatshirt (sent to her by her grandma from the

States) was an "actual Tommy Hilfiger"—not that I ever knew what that meant or even cared.

But I soon discover the "clearance" racks, where everything is kind of mixed up (not unlike the trash-and-treasure sales we sometimes have at the mission to raise money for special events). I really have to search for the right sizes, but it doesn't take long before I start unearthing some really cool bargains. I just about shout "Hallelujah!" when I find a terrific-looking pink polo shirt for only $3.99! And then another just like it in pale blue. And then I find some nice black trousers for only $6.99 and a khaki skirt for $8.99, and I honestly think I've died and gone to bargain heaven. It's not long before I realize why I needed this trolley, because by the time I finish up in the clearance section, it's heaped with all sorts of things. And not only "work" clothes. I also found some bathers—rather, a *bikini*—that I think looks a lot like what Vanessa wears. I know my parents won't approve of so much skin exposure, and we're not allowed to wear anything but one-piece bathers at the mission, but both these bikini pieces are only $15.99 together, and even if I only wear it this summer, I think it might be worth it.

As I wheel my noisy trolley back to the sign that says Dressing Rooms, which I assume must be change rooms, I reckon I've done pretty well. I've not only selected some sensible work clothes, but I've also collected a few pieces that are a bit like some things I've seen Vanessa wearing. And I'm hoping that I'll emerge with some outfits that won't embarrass Vanessa and my aunt. To be perfectly honest, I'm hoping I'll come out looking as stylish as Vanessa, but at a fraction of the cost. I have allotted myself $150 today, so it won't be easy.

"Only eight items," says the short, dark-skinned woman in charge of the change rooms. Her name tag says Mridula, and I'm guessing she's from India.

41

I look at my heaped trolley and then back at her. "You mean I can only purchase eight items?" I ask. "That doesn't seem quite—"

"You can buy the whole cart if you want, but you can only try on eight items at a time."

"Oh." So I quickly grab eight pieces of work attire, take the plastic number that she hands me, and make my way back to the crowded change rooms. I hear women talking and laughing back there. Several speak different languages, but then I'm used to that. For some reason it comforts me that Southern California has so many different cultures. Maybe it's because I'm reminded that I'm not the only one here who might feel like a reffo.

I slowly work my way through the pile, going back and forth to the Indian woman and taking back eight items at a time until I've finally decided on several suitable work outfits, the orange-and-turquoise bikini, two pairs of shorts, a short denim skirt, some just-for-fun T-shirts, and what I heard another girl calling a "tank top." I mentally tally the total and realize that I am barely at $100—about half the price of Vanessa's Prada T-shirt. And I realize, as I wheel my thumpity trolley through the crowded shop, that I may actually be gloating. I glance around, checking to see if Vanessa has returned, but I still don't see her anywhere. However, I notice her three mates, or rather ex-mates, standing over in a section that seems to be for shoes.

Shoes? I hadn't even considered this. So I head on over and it's not long before I've found a pair of pale pink rubber thongs for only $4.99, and they even have sparkles on them! And then I find some nice leather sandals that I reckon will be good for work, as well as a pair of shoes that are open like clogs in the back that I hear a woman calling "mules." I think it's funny to name shoes after a mule, but they are very comfortable, and the woman tells me that they go well with pants. So I decide to get them. And as I am leaving the shoe section, I come across the purse section.

Can you believe it? There is a pink plastic purse that looks identical to the Prada one that Vanessa so proudly brags about, and despite myself, I am pulled in. I pick up the shiny bag and examine it closely, and although I don't see the name Prada on it anywhere, I cannot decide if it's real or not. It sure looks authentic to me. Then I notice a similar purse, only this one is orange—the same color orange as one of my new T-shirts. I decide to check the price and cannot believe that the tag is marked down to only $9.99. Why not? After all, when in Rome, do as the Romans do, right?

So I toss the bright orange purse into my trolley and head for the cash registers, still glancing around to see if Vanessa has come back. But I think she plans to lay low until her old mates shoot through and consequently make the coast clear for her. I glance at my watch, and by LA time, I have spent only a little over an hour here—about a third of the time that Vanessa managed to waste yesterday—and yet I have about ten times as many items as she bought, at just a fraction of the cost. To say I'm feeling quite pleased with myself is a bit of an understatement. As I set my purchases on the counter, I forget myself and slip into my old Aussie greeting and say, "G'day!" to the middle-aged Asian checkout chick. She looks at me curiously but just starts adding up my purchases, then finally proclaims, "$148.76."

I extract the strange-looking green notes from my wallet and carefully count them all out, hoping I got the right ones since they all look almost identical to me. "I think that's right," I tell her.

She looks at me curiously. "Where are you from?"

"Papua New Guinea," I tell her, waiting for her reaction. Most people don't even know where it is, so I usually have to explain that it's the largest island in the South Pacific and is near Australia.

"My mother used to live there," she says in a matter-of-fact voice.

"*Really?*"

She nods as she hands me my change.

"Her family left mainland China during the war. Somehow they ended up in New Guinea afterward. They ran a shop in Port Moresby. Some of them are still there."

I smile at her, then reach across the counter to shake her hand. "It's a small world."

She returns my smile as she bags up my purchases. "Yes, I guess it is."

As I'm telling her good-bye, I see Vanessa rock up. Still wearing her lime-green sunnies, she discretely glances around. I yell her name and wave.

She gives me that look, the one that suggests I am doing the wrong thing once again. So, pretending to act like a spy, I creep toward the door with my bulging gray plastic bags in hand, glancing over both shoulders before I whisper, "I think it's safe to leave now."

She makes a noise that suggests she's fed up and then darts out the door like a cut snake. I hope I haven't made her too mad. "Wait, Vanessa," I yell after her. "I'm sorry."

She turns and looks at me now, temptingly holding out a big mocha frappé. "You act like *that* . . . and after I got this for you?"

"Sorry," I say again. "I didn't mean to start a row with you."

She almost smiles now. "Okay, here's your frappé. I hope it's not all melted."

"Thanks." I unlock the Jeep and toss my packages into the back, pausing to dig through a lumpy plastic sack.

"What are you looking for?"

"I want to put on my new thongs."

"Right here?"

"Huh?" I finally unearth the sparkly pink thongs and hold them up.

"*Flip-flops*," she says in a corrective voice. "Those are called *flip-flops*, Hannah. I've already told you that like a hundred times. Flip-flops go on your feet, and thongs are underwear."

"You thought I was going to change my knickers right here in the parking lot?" Now it is my turn to laugh. Of course, I don't mention that I don't even own any "thongs" or that I reckon they're the skimpiest excuse for knickers imaginable.

Now she's poking around my packages with curiosity. "What else did you get, Hannah?"

"Clothes," I say happily. "Lots and lots of clothes. But let's jet. I can show them to you when we get home."

She groans as we get into the hot Jeep. "This cannot be good," she says as she buckles up. "No way can this be good."

five

As IT TURNS OUT, VANESSA ISN'T TERRIBLY IMPRESSED WITH MY NEW clothes. Neither is my aunt when she comes home from her lunch date. I ask them what the problem is, but their answers are vague, and they seem slightly embarrassed for me, as if they reckon I'm a bogan or a plain old no-hoper.

"I just don't understand what's wrong with these things." I hold up a T-shirt that looks a bit like the one Vanessa is wearing right this minute.

"Besides *everything*?" Vanessa drops my new orange purse as if it's a hot potato. It lands with a thump on the pile of clothing that's heaped on the sectional.

"Oh, they're not that bad," says Aunt Lori in what I'm sure she thinks is a consoling tone, although I think it's patronizing. "And the clothes you got for work should be just fine."

"But really," I persist. "What's wrong with the others? Like this purse, for instance." I pick up the cast-off orange bag that's actually beginning to grow on me and loop it over my arm as if I'm going somewhere.

"It's a cheap knock-off," says Vanessa. "Anyone can see that."

"What's a knock-off?" I ask.

"An imitation of the real thing."

"Oh." Then I set my purse on the coffee table next to her purse and am amazed at how similar they look. "I just can't see it," I say.

She points out some imperceptible details and then just shrugs as if I'm hopeless. "It's not your fault, Hannah. It takes time to develop an eye for these things."

To be honest, I think if the items I purchased had overpriced tags and were wrapped in fine tissue and tucked into fancy bags, no one would be the wiser. But maybe I'm really confused.

Now Vanessa is flipping through the telly channels, so I decide to collect my purchases and stow them in my room before my stylish cousin deems them suitable for the rubbish bin. But while I'm in my room, I hold up the items of clothing, one by one, and peer at them in the mirror. Maybe I am a complete loser, but I honestly think they look alright. And I wonder what the big deal is anyway. Maybe Vanessa is just jealous that I got so much for such a good price. Who knows? So I decide to put on my new bathers—rather, my *bikini* —and take the shark book down to the pool and just kick back. My midsection, while long and trim, is painfully pale—the color of milk. I don't think this part of my anatomy has *ever* seen the light of day. Even more reason to head for the pool and get some sun.

I swim for a bit, then zonk out on a lounge chair until I wake up and discover that my tummy is getting fairly well baked. I press my finger into the spot just above my belly button and see a white spot emerge beneath the pink. Not a very good sign. I'm afraid I've gotten rather burned.

I put a shirt on, wrap the towel like a skirt around my legs, and head over to a side yard that I recently discovered. It's like a tiny secret garden where this lovely vine with purple flowers climbs over a trellis. The trellis covers the tiny stone patio and a concrete bench tucked into the corner. It's cool and shady and perfect for reading.

I've actually convinced myself that no one really knows about this place. Well, other than the yardman. Every square inch of this yard is maintained to absolute perfection. Before long I am lost in the shark adventure again.

"Aren't you going to the birthday party with Vanessa?" my aunt asks, making me jump and breaking the peaceful silence of my little getaway. I look up from my book to see my aunt's concerned face looking down at me.

"What's that?" I ask, as if I haven't heard that Elisa is having her seventeenth birthday party tonight.

"Aren't you going with Vanessa tonight?"

I shrug. "Not that I'm aware of."

"Well, Ron and I are having a few friends over . . . I suppose you could join us if you'd like."

"No," I say quickly. "I'm good on my own. I can just read in my room or something."

She frowns now. "I'm going to speak to Vanessa."

"Nah, it's cool," I begin, but she is already leaving, and now I'm getting a bit cheesed off. I hate feeling like I'm such a bother to everyone, and I wonder yet again why my parents had to go and dump me here in the first place.

Finally I decide that it's no use to worry about things I cannot change, and so I go back to the shark book. I'm nearly finished with it and want to find out if the cocky fisherman is going to become dinner for the shark or not.

I'm just reading the last page when Vanessa makes an appearance, but I hold up my hand for her to wait as I finish the last couple of paragraphs. "The shark won," I tell her, closing the book and looking up to see her wearing her expensive blue T-shirt and a short skirt just a few shades darker.

"Well, you certainly scrub up nicely," I say brightly. "Have fun at Elisa's birthday party."

"That's why I'm here. Mom thinks I should take you along—"

"I told her that I was fine on my own."

"It's not that I don't want you to come," she continues. "But I'm worried you'll feel . . . well, you know, left out."

"Right. I don't expect your mates to take me in just because I'm your cousin. I know how it works."

Now she frowns. "Oh, what does it matter? Okay, I've changed my mind. I think you should come with me tonight. I was just being paranoid. There's no reason my friends can't accept you for who you are, Hannah."

I wonder what that's supposed to mean. And then I wonder who I am, as Vanessa sees me.

"Seriously, Hannah." She's pulling on my hand now. "Get up and get changed. Hurry. I need to stop by the mall and pick out a gift for Elisa."

"But I—"

"No arguing. Mom's already mad at me."

"But I don't want—"

"Don't make this any harder than it is. Go and get cleaned up. You have exactly twenty minutes. And wear something . . ." She pauses. "Well, something that looks sort of normal."

Sort of normal? What's that supposed to mean?

So I trudge upstairs, and feeling sorry for myself, I take a very fast shower, then search through my new clothes until I come up with an outfit that not only looks normal but is rather attractive. I put on the orange T-shirt and a black skirt that's probably a more suitable length for work than a party, but I don't have anything like the skirt that Vanessa was wearing. Then I pull my hair back into a damp ponytail and put on some lip gloss and quickly transfer my wallet and things into the new orange purse. I go back and forth between the pink thongs, I mean flip-flops, and sandals and finally decide on the sandals since I think pink and orange are a bit gross together. Then I check out my image in the mirror once more, and I think I look pretty good.

Vanessa is waiting in her room, just down the hall from mine, with the door open. I'm pretty sure I made my transformation within her allotted amount of time, but she still doesn't look happy when she sees me.

"Getting ready for Halloween, are we?"

"Huh?"

"The orange and black thing you got going . . . it looks kind of like Halloween."

"You mean like trick-or-treat?"

"Yeah, right." Then she goes over to her dresser and digs through some of her costume jewelry until she finds some big black beads and matching earrings. "Here," she tells me. "Try this."

I put on the necklace, then remind her my ears aren't pierced.

She frowns again. "Yeah, we should do something about that." Then she glances at her watch, a thin piece of silver that looks more like jewelry than an actual watch. "We better go."

Vanessa drives, and rather fast. We stop at the same mall that she took me to on Friday and go straight to a store with a French name that I can't pronounce. Vanessa seems to know just what she's looking for, and it occurs to me that I should take the birthday girl something too. The problem is, I'm almost out of cash and I don't want to sponge off of Vanessa. Finally I decide on a card and hope that it will be sufficient. After all, I've barely even met Elisa.

I feel myself growing nervous as we drive up a road that leads to a neighborhood that's even more posh than where Vanessa lives. I wipe my damp palms on my skirt and wish that I had simply stayed home. Why did I allow Vanessa to push me around? I know better than to be egged on into doing something that I'll regret later. But to be perfectly honest, a small part of me wanted to go to this party tonight. I'm curious about Yanks my age. I wonder if they all share Vanessa's superficial values or if she's just been overly influenced by her materialistic mum.

"Just relax," Vanessa coaches me as she parks in the huge circular driveway. "Be yourself, and I'm sure everyone will be charmed by your Aussie accent."

"Ya reckon?"

She laughs. "Sure, why not?"

As it turns out, they are a bit interested in me. For starters anyway. But then they start drifting off into little groups, and I am not included. I find a quiet corner out by the pool. Me and pools, what is it? I guess I like water and find it to be soothing company. Doesn't talk too much and keeps its cool.

But as I sit there, I observe the others. And one thing becomes clear: These kids all seem to have a lot of money. I can tell this (a) by the way they're dressed, (b) by the way they talk (everyone's been or going somewhere this summer that sounds pretty expensive), and (c) by the amazing cars parked in the driveway. But more than this, I can tell that I do not fit in. Vanessa was absolutely right. And I can't even blame her for not wanting to bring me. What's the point? Oh, I was an item of interest for a few brief moments, and I must admit that was fun. But now that my fifteen seconds of fame are over, I wish that I hadn't bothered coming at all. Sitting here by myself is just a giant reminder of what a misfit I truly am.

But as I sit here, I notice something else that's interesting. Vanessa is by no means at the top of this money heap. In fact, some of her own mates don't seem to treat her that nicely. And then it occurs to me that she's a bit of a newcomer to the whole wealth thing. Only six years ago she was just a regular middle-class girl. The more I watch, the more I suspect she has to fight to keep her position, and I find this both pitiful and amusing.

"What are you doing over here all by yourself?" asks a guy I met earlier. His name is Wyatt, and he's quite good-looking with his short, bleached hair and deep tan. He already told me he's a surfer.

"Just having a breather," I say as if I'm staying off to myself by choice.

"That's cool." He sits down in the chair across from me and leans back as if he wants to take a break as well.

"How often do you surf?" I ask, feeling more like a boofhead than ever. What a completely idiotic question.

"As much as I can," he says. "Especially this summer."

"Why especially this summer?" I echo stupidly, but he doesn't seem to notice my lack of verbal skills.

"I'm going to college back East." His voice grows sad. "No surfing there."

"That's too bad."

"Do you surf?"

"I've done it on occasion, but I'm not very good."

"Maybe you should try hanging ten here. We may not be Australia, but we get some pretty good wave action. The waves were epic yesterday. You should come out and see how we Yanks do it." I wonder if this might actually be an offer for surfing lessons, and I'm about to respond accordingly when I'm cut off.

"*Wyatt!*" A girl waves from the other side of the pool. As I recall, her name is Felicia VanHorn, and from what I've seen, she must rank fairly high on the social ladder of Vanessa's mates. "What are you doing way over there?"

"Talking to the Aussie girl, Hannah," he calls back.

"Oh, *Hannah* . . ." says Felicia as she comes over to join us. She says my name as if I'm some sort of specimen that she's been wanting to examine. "I didn't even see you there in the shadows. Must be those dark colors you're wearing." Then she pulls up a chair and sits down beside Wyatt. "Are those colors the fashion Down Under?"

Felicia is wearing a loopy top that seems to have been crocheted or knitted, yet it's very lightweight and the same delicate shade of pink that you might see inside a seashell. It fits her like a glove and yet doesn't look the slightest bit shonky. Her short skirt is the exact same shell color, and I can tell the two pieces must've been purchased as an outfit. Her clothes are perfectly accented with jewelry that suggests the ocean and looks striking against her tanned skin.

I look down at my orange and black outfit and remember what Vanessa said about Halloween (a holiday we don't normally observe on the mission), then simply shrug. "We don't get all worked up over fashion where I'm from," I say, hoping I sound more confident than I feel. "I reckon it's 'cause we focus more on *doing* things."

"What kinds of things?" asks Wyatt.

"Well, besides surfing, there are field sports and motorbikes and walkabouts and goomying."

"Goomying?" Felicia looks confused.

"Oh, you know, floating on tire tubes downriver."

Felicia looks surprised or maybe disgusted. And I cannot for the life of me imagine someone like her getting all dirty and mucked up as we shoot down the river. But I think it would be interesting to see.

"Sounds fun," says Wyatt. "Any crocs in your rivers?"

"Oh, sure. We've spotted some really big crocs down in the lower elevations. And we've got after darks in the ocean too."

"What's that?"

"*Sharks.*" I say the word dramatically since I know he's a surfer.

"Oh, we have sharks around here," says Felicia, perhaps to show me up.

"And we also have pythons and boas." I try to think of something even more exciting, as if I'm participating in some kind of who's-got-the-best-wildlife contest.

"Cool," says Wyatt. And he actually seems impressed.

"You should pop over sometime," I tease.

"That'd be gnarly."

Felicia slowly crosses her long, brown legs, then points her perfectly painted toes, gracefully encased in a fancy beaded sandal, in Wyatt's direction. It's obvious she's trying to get his attention, but I'm wondering if she expects him to rub her feet. "My dad's taking out the sailboat tomorrow," she says to Wyatt as if I'm not here. "He told me to round up some able-bodied crew members."

"Where's he going?" Wyatt asks with interest.

"Just to Catalina and back. But we could use an extra hand."

Suddenly I feel invisible as the two of them discuss the details of the sailing trip. I would get up and slink away except that I don't want to draw any undue attention to myself. But as I sit here watching them, I can't help but notice how perfectly turned out Felicia is. I have a feeling her outfit might've cost even more than Vanessa's. And for some reason I'm beginning to see how money and influence and the ability to come and go and do as you please really matter with this crowd.

Finally, when I can't handle being ignored for one more second, I stand up and excuse myself. Wyatt looks slightly surprised by my quick move, but I suspect Felicia is relieved. I have a feeling that my outfit was clashing with hers. Most of all, I reckon Vanessa was right. I don't belong here. I decide to go into the house, although I'm not even sure why. But then I just continue walking, as if I know where I am going, until I'm finally out in the front yard. I stand there for about a minute stupidly staring at all the beautiful vehicles lining Elisa's driveway. *Yank tanks* . . . although most of them do not appear to be American made. I am tempted to tally up the value of all the metal spread out before me, but instead I just go and sit on a concrete bench that surrounds a tall fountain and wait. And wait and wait and wait.

six

THE HUGEST LUMP IS GROWING IN MY THROAT RIGHT NOW, AND I FEEL like the biggest misfit in the whole wide world. Not only that, but I am jealous too. And jealousy isn't something I'm accustomed to. Back home at the mission, I'm considered the kind of girl that others normally look up to. I'm good at sports and have heaps of mates. I excel in my studies, and my teachers often refer to me as "a leader." I think I've simply taken that role in stride, as if being first and best was somehow my due. But here in the States, the rules have all changed. It's plain to see that in the wider world, I am a big fat nothing. And that hurts.

I replay the scene of Felicia flirting with Wyatt and honestly wish that I were in her shoes. Literally. Those delicately beaded sandals were absolutely beautiful, like jewelry for the feet. And her feet were beautiful too with those pale pink toenails. I look down at my unimpressive sturdy leather sandals that I actually purchased for work, and then I examine my scruffy-looking feet and my plain-Jane toenails, which are in need of a trim. I've never even considered my toenails before tonight. Painting them has always seemed sort of cheap and wasteful to me. But suddenly I'm asking myself, why not?

"Mind if I smoke?" asks a bloke I don't recognize from the party. I hadn't even noticed him walking up to me, but now he's standing with one foot on the bench. He's got dark, shaggy hair and a goatee that doesn't quite seem to fit his face.

"It's a free country," I say, watching as he slides a cancer stick in his gob, then ignites it with a lighter.

"You a friend of Elisa's?" he asks with undisguised curiosity.

"Not actually."

"Who, then?" He blows a puff of smoke over his shoulder and away from me.

"Vanessa Johnson's my cousin," I explain for what I'm hoping will be the last time. I want to say, "Yeah, I know I look like I don't belong here tonight. And you're right, I don't!" But somehow I manage to keep my mouth shut.

"Doesn't look like you're having much fun."

"I'm not, actually. I'm just waiting for the party to end so I can go home."

"Might be a long wait."

I shrug and glance back toward the house. It does sound as if the party is just getting lively now.

The guy comes closer to me and holds out his hand as if he wants to shake mine. "Sorry, I'm Alex Rodriguez. I'm Elisa's older brother. I just came by to tell her happy birthday, but I'm not really into these kiddie parties either."

I shake his hand and eye him more carefully. I realize that he doesn't quite look like the other guys here tonight, although I'm sure I can't put my finger on why. But then, I'm not exactly known for my fashion sense, am I? I wonder if he is what Vanessa would call a nerd, or what my mates and I would call a dag. And then I wonder why it even matters. Why must we label everything?

"I could give you a ride home," he offers. "I mean, if you're tired of waiting. I'm just leaving anyway."

I don't feel right about hopping into this bloke's car. For all I know, he could be some murderer who's just popping in to pick up his next victim. But then I think if he's really Elisa's brother, he should be safe enough. Even so, I decide to check with Vanessa first. She glances at Alex, who waits for me by the door. Then she gives me this odd look and lowers her voice and says, "It's perfectly fine if he takes you home, Hannah, if you're not embarrassed to be seen with him. Alex is kind of a dork—you know, a loser. But a harmless one."

Dork, geek, nerd, dag, loser, wally . . . so many clever names for us misfits. I don't reckon we'll ever run out.

"I'm alright," I assure Vanessa, but I'm thinking she may be more worried about how my leaving with Alex will reflect on her. "I don't think anyone will notice us anyway."

And as I get into the passenger side of his small pickup, I realize that I was right—no one noticed us leaving. No one even cared. I guess I really hoped that Wyatt would look up and see me going—that perhaps he might dash over and ask for my phone number or invite me to go surfing with him next week. But he was still talking to Felicia. And she was laughing loudly, as if he'd just said the funniest thing. Maybe it was about me. Or maybe he'd already forgotten me.

"You have an accent," Alex says as he pulls out into the street.

So I quickly explain, giving him my formula answer and hoping that will be sufficient. I do appreciate the ride, but I have no interest in carrying on an actual conversation with this bloke. I just tell him the address of Vanessa's house, then lean back into the seat and hope he doesn't get lost.

"Elisa's friends aren't an easy circle to break into."

I attempt a laugh. "No worries," I say. "I have no intention of *breaking* in. I only went tonight because my aunt forced Vanessa to take me. She's afraid I'm not enjoying my visit."

"Are you?"

"Not a lot."

"Elisa and her friends are really obsessed with money."

Now this makes me actually laugh. Talk about stating the obvious. "No kidding?"

He clears his throat and now I'm worried I may have offended him. "I guess it's not money so much as the lifestyle that goes with it," he continues. "The funny thing is that none of them even work. They just spend their parents' money—as if there's no end to it." Now his tone sounds slightly bitter.

"But you don't do that?"

"Elisa and I have different dads. Oh, I have the Rodriguez name; my mom insisted on it when I was too small to protest. But Elisa's dad is the one with the money. My dad is pretty much a loser."

"I'm sorry."

He shakes his head. "Don't be. I'm not. I just realize that I need to work harder than Elisa to make something of myself."

"You mean to get rich?"

"I'm not into money."

Somehow I don't believe this. "Everyone's into money," I say. "You can't live without it."

"Well, I want to live differently. After graduating from high school, I moved out, and I haven't taken a penny from my stepdad since. I work hard just to get by. And I don't waste my money on the kinds of things that Elisa and her friends are into."

"How can you afford uni?"

"Uni?"

"I mean college, you know. Have you gone yet?"

"I took a few classes the first year, just part-time, but I can't afford to go. I have to stay focused on work."

"Do you enjoy your work?"

"No. But I enjoy having food to eat and a roof over my head."

Now, I don't even know why I'm drawn into this conversation. What do I care if this bloke has family problems? I have enough troubles of my own. But I plunge ahead. "Are you jealous of Elisa for having it so easy?"

"It's not her fault that she has it easy, that her dad just hands her everything on a silver platter. It's not like she has a choice in the matter. And besides, she's going to find out someday that money doesn't buy happiness."

"Are you happy?"

He doesn't answer, and I begin to feel bad for pestering him. After all, this guy is giving me a ride home. Why am I being so mean?

"Sorry," I say. "It's none of my business."

Now he brightens a bit. "No, you ask good questions, Hannah. I guess I haven't really thought about everything. Sometimes I get pretty obsessed with working and getting by."

"You seem like an intelligent person," I say. "Don't you want to go to uni—I mean college?"

"Of course, I want to go. I'm just not sure how to make it work."

"And you won't ask your stepdad for help?"

He firmly shakes his head. "Never."

"That's the house," I say suddenly, surprised that we're already here. "Thanks for the ride." I'm reaching for the door handle, eager to get out of this rather sticky conversation.

"You seem like a level-headed girl, Hannah. It's been a pleasure talking to you."

I don't know why his words surprise me, but I simply nod and thank him again for the ride. "I hope things work out for you," I say before I close the door.

As I walk up to the house, I feel sorry for Alex. And then I realize that Alex and I are not so very different, and that makes me angry. I'm not even sure why I feel so angry, but I don't think I want to be identified with someone like him, a "loser" as Vanessa put it. I do not want to be a loser.

I tiptoe through the foyer and up the stairs. I can hear the sounds of music and voices back toward the great room, but I don't want them to hear me. I don't want to interrupt their fun. Instead I go to my room, shut the door, and sit down on the bed and just cry. I think it's stupid to cry. Not to mention a complete waste of time. But I can't help myself. I feel so lost and hopeless right now. And confused.

I consider that I have only one year of school left at the mission, and then I'll be expected to return to the States for uni. In fact, my parents have hinted that I should consider remaining here for my last year of school so that I can have resident status to help with my tuition next year. But I told them I don't want to do this, that I want to go back to New Guinea and graduate with my mates. And while the idea of going home brings some consolation, especially now, I feel slightly terrified to realize that it's not long before I will have to come back to the States—where I am a loser and a reffo and a misfit—and I will have to stay here permanently. This thought alone makes me cry even harder.

I throw myself across my bed and cry until my pillow is thoroughly soaked. Then I sit up. I am normally not a crier. I learned early on that criers and complainers don't get on so well at the group home. We call them sooks or babies and expect them to shape up or suffer the consequences. The truth is, I've always considered myself to be made of fairly tough stuff. But not tonight. I vaguely wonder if I might be hormonal, or maybe I'm going loony or possibly suffering from low blood sugar because I didn't get enough to eat. I felt a bit awkward eating in front of all those strangers tonight. Or else I'm just making excuses.

I'm dying to pop downstairs and sneak into the pool. I can imagine how the cool water would soothe and cool my overheated face and puffy eyes, as well as my sunburned belly, but I don't want to intrude on the party. I slip down the hallway a bit, just to listen and see if the partygoers are still down there making merry. Unfortunately, they are.

I walk past Vanessa's room, noticing that the door's slightly ajar, and so I stop for a moment, just standing there and staring like a boofhead. Then I just walk right in. I don't even know why I'm doing this, and I actually feel a bit guilty. Her room has never been off-bounds for me, and she's always made me feel welcome. Even so, I feel like a trespasser. Just the same, I keep going. I walk around and casually look at everything.

I pause when I see some pieces of jewelry scattered on top of her dresser. I'm reminded that I'm wearing Vanessa's necklace, which actually gives me a good excuse to be in her room. I take it off and set it on her dresser. Then, instead of leaving as I should, I look around a bit more. I feel as if I'm playing detective now, as if I might discover some sort of clue for why Vanessa is the way she is, but everything in here looks pretty much the same as always. For the most part, Vanessa keeps things rather tidy (or maybe that's the work of Consuela), but I do notice a haphazard pile of clothes on the floor of her closet. I suspect they're things she tried on for the party before deciding that her expensive Prada shirt was the right choice. And she did get some compliments on that top too. What do I know anyway?

I pick a pale blue blouse from the top of Vanessa's discard pile and hold it up in front of me. Standing in front of the mirror on her closet door, I imagine that I am wearing this blouse. But it looks odd against the bright orange of my T-shirt beneath it. And so I remove my bargain T-shirt and carefully slip the blouse on and button it up. The sleeves are a bit short, but other than that, it actually fits rather well. I suspect the fabric is silk. It feels cool, almost like water, to my skin, especially against my sunburned belly. But this is what I really find interesting: I look like a completely different person in this blouse. I'm not sure how to define it exactly, but it's sort of refined and classy and, of course, rich. It's almost as if this blouse contains some kind of magic. Or maybe I'm delusional after my crying fit. Or perhaps it's the lighting in here. I examine my reflection from various positions, but the blouse looks absolutely perfect from every angle.

Then I slowly remove this spectacular blouse and almost reverently hang it on a padded hanger. I notice that the tag inside says MIU MIU, not that those strange words mean anything to me—well, other than *expensive* because I'm sure that it is. But I carefully hang it on the rod and put my orange T-shirt back on, which suddenly looks harsh and somewhat garish and, I must admit, *cheap*.

As I creep back to my room, I hear the clock chiming downstairs. Eleven o'clock and all is well. All except for me, that is. I feel anything but well as I remove my clothes and climb into bed. It seems my world is being turned upside down, and I have absolutely no control over anything anymore. I feel small and insignificant, and I'm not even sure why.

seven

APPARENTLY NO ONE IN THIS FAMILY GOES TO CHURCH ON SUNDAYS, OR any other day for that matter. And so I decide that I'm not going to make the effort either. In fact, following my cousin's example, I manage to sleep in this morning—only until nine, but it's a small accomplishment nonetheless. Or maybe just an escape.

"Are we still on for shopping?" asks Aunt Lori later in the morning.

"Shopping?" I echo as I pour myself a second cup of coffee, then add milk and sugar.

"Yes, you and me and Vanessa are going shopping today—to get you some things, Hannah. Surely you didn't forget about it."

I shrug. "It's not so much that I forgot . . ." I consider how to put this. "But the truth is, I spent most of my money yesterday, and until I get paid for working for Uncle—"

"No no," says Aunt Lori. "You must've misunderstood me. This is my treat. I want to take my favorite niece shopping—just for fun."

"I'm your only niece."

"You're still my favorite. How about if we leave here around noon? We can shop a little, then get some lunch, and then we'll shop until we drop."

So it is that we pile into Aunt Lori's Audi and head for a shopping center. As she promised, it's not the same mall that Vanessa took me to on Friday. Anyway, the name is different. But if you ask me, they look quite similar. And the disturbing thing is that there seem to be lots and lots of them.

I feel like I'm about seven years old as I sit in the backseat, listening to Vanessa and Aunt Lori discussing what might or might not look good on me. They are such experts. But before long they're disagreeing over something to do with pants, and just when it sounds as if they're going to have a fight over which designer is best, Aunt Lori pulls into an empty parking space, and I thankfully hop out of the car and stretch my arms and legs.

I look down at my outfit and hope that I don't look too "lame," as Vanessa puts it. I must've changed my clothes about ten times before I finally settled on something that I hoped wouldn't humiliate my aunt and cousin and, as it turns out, myself as well. It seems that something in me is finally becoming somewhat fashion conscious. Anyway, I am wearing my pink polo shirt and a khaki skirt and my pink thongs. I have my hair pulled back in a ponytail, and I think I look fairly respectable, but that's about it.

"Now, you've got to be open," Aunt Lori tells me as we enter the mall. "You need to be willing to try new things, Hannah."

I shrug. "I'll do my best."

"And don't worry about the cost of everything," says Vanessa. "The important thing is to make sure it looks good on you."

"I'm not a very good judge of that," I admit.

"That's why we're here, dear." Aunt Lori pats me on the back. "Just trust us, and everything will be fine."

So it is that I deliver myself into the hands of these two well-meaning shopping divas. As we peruse the sleek chrome racks and glass shelves, I'm fascinated by how Aunt Lori and Vanessa know their way around the various shops. And not only can they pronounce the names of every single designer, they can recognize some of their works simply by the style and cut of a garment. It's all quite mysterious to me. Like speaking a lost language or knowing a secret handshake.

And so I just let them lead me around by the nose. I try on what they tell me to try on and then emerge from the change room and stand out in the open like a mannequin while they inspect and critique my outfit. After a while I begin to pretend that I'm not really here or that it's someone else wearing my skin and these strange items of clothing. And it's almost as if I can't hear them going back and forth about what looks better than what. I almost feel that I'm in a dream.

"Maybe it's her hair," says Vanessa as she circles me with a scrutinizing expression. She reaches up and releases it from its barrette, fluffing it out with her fingers. "Although the texture's not bad."

Aunt Lori stands up and moves closer. "I think you're on to something." Then she seems to be studying my hair. "The cut's not doing anything for her."

"Nope."

"And it doesn't have much color, does it?"

Vanessa just grimly shakes her head.

"You know," says the salesgirl, as if she's been invited to criticize my hair too, "my sister's hair is naturally that color too, but she had it tinted this red shade, and I couldn't believe the difference."

"Red?" says Aunt Lori with interest.

"No chance," I tell them, snapping to attention. I've got to draw the line somewhere, and this is it. "I might wear some of these clothes you're picking out for me, but I will *not* become a bluey."

The salesgirl laughs. "Her accent is so cute."

"What's a *bluey*?" asks Vanessa as she flops down in one of the waiting chairs and reaches for a thick *Vogue* magazine.

"Someone with *red* hair," I snap. "Someone that's not me."

"I'm not suggesting *red* hair," says the salesgirl pleasantly. "My sister's hair is kind of a golden red. I'm not sure what she calls it, but it's pretty."

"I can see that on Hannah," says Aunt Lori. "I think it would go nicely with your green eyes. And wasn't Grandma Johnson a redhead before she went gray? I've heard people in the family saying that you resemble her a lot. I think you should try it."

"You don't have to use permanent color," says the salesgirl.

"I don't have to use *any* color," I shoot back.

"Just consider it, Hannah." Then Aunt Lori turns to the salesgirl. "I think we'll take the Armani pants that she's wearing. And did you set that yellow Fendi top aside for us?"

"Yes, it looked great on her."

"How about the jeans?" asks Vanessa. "Let's get her those Diesel jeans too. Maybe I can borrow them and just cuff them up."

"If you can get them buttoned," teases Aunt Lori.

"Thanks a lot, Mom." Vanessa growls as she turns her attention back to the magazine.

Finally we stop for lunch. Vanessa is still pouting over her mom's comment about buttoning the jeans and consequently orders a salad with light dressing. I'm starved and go for the pasta special.

"Show-off," says Vanessa after the waiter leaves.

"Huh?"

"Never mind." She rolls her eyes and looks away.

Aunt Lori is trying to reach someone on her cell phone and seems to be stuck on hold before she suddenly gets through. And I can tell by her conversation that she's trying to make a hair appointment for me.

"I know, Celia, but she works during the day," Aunt Lori says in a pleading voice. "I just thought maybe you could do me this huge favor and squeeze her in." She pauses, listening. "Really? Oh, Celia, that'd be great. Thank you so much! You're the best!" Then she closes her phone and turns triumphantly to me. "You've got an appointment."

"But I don't want—"

"No arguing. Celia is squeezing you in this afternoon at four."

"Do I have to go too?" asks Vanessa.

"No, we'll drop you off at home."

"But I really don't need to—"

"Hannah," says Aunt Lori in a stern voice. "I said no arguing." Then she smiles. "Just wait, you're going to thank me for this."

I try not to imagine myself with flaming red hair as the waiter sets our orders before us. Then I wonder why I even care. I won't be seeing any of my mates for nearly six months anyway. Maybe I should just give it a go. And if it turns out horribly, it will at least be grown out or faded by the time I'm back in school.

We shop a bit more after lunch. The focus now seems to be shoes and accessories. And I can't really complain since the shoes they pick are actually quite nice. They're sandals made by Tod's (which at least sounds fairly normal), and they are also very nice looking and not as uncomfortable as some of the shoes I've tried on. They pick out some accessories to go with the clothes we've already gotten. I've started to lose track now, but Aunt Lori and Vanessa seem to have it all locked into their pretty little heads. And I'm so weary that I just nod and agree and hope we can end this thing soon. I have no idea how much Aunt Lori has spent on me, and I have decided I don't even care. If they're so wealthy that they can waste money like that, well, what's it to me? Besides, I actually like most of the things they've selected. And I must admit that I looked pretty awesome in some of them, despite their opinions of my hair.

I think I've been worn down. I think it may be part of Aunt Lori's plan. But after we drop off Vanessa, I get to ride in the front seat, and I lean back and feel thankful that we're not trekking around the mall anymore. At least I get to sit for a while.

"I didn't think hairdressers worked on Sundays," I say as Aunt Lori pulls into a parking lot that's behind some businesses.

"Fantasia's does."

"Fantasia? Like the old Disney movie?" I imagine myself emerging from my hair appointment looking like some kind of Walt Disney Ariel, flaming red hair and all.

"Trust me," says Aunt Lori. "Both Vanessa and I come here all the time."

I glance at Aunt Lori and realize that she's quite a good advertisement for this place. She looks absolutely perfect with every hair and nail and whatnot in place. Maybe there's hope for me too.

We wait for about fifteen minutes before a woman in her thirties comes to get me. "I'm Celia," she says. "You must be Hannah."

Aunt Lori follows us back to Celia's station, talking the whole time about what kind of cut and color she thinks will best suit me. And once again, I let the words flow in one ear and out the next.

Finally Aunt Lori seems to have run out of advice and goes back to the waiting area.

"Just relax," says Celia as she gently shampoos my hair, even though I tell her I washed it this morning. So I try to take her advice and relax, and it's not long before I'm starting to think that this kind of pampering and attention isn't so bad. In fact, I'm beginning to feel rather special.

"I'm going to do a razor cut," she announces as she holds up what looks like a surgical tool.

"What?" I ask, jerking myself back to attention. "I thought you were going to cut my hair."

She laughs. "I am. But I'm going to use a razor so that I can do some shaping, texturizing, and layering. Just relax."

"Right." That's when I decide to shut my eyes. There seems no point in getting all worked up about something I have no control over. Like my life.

I suspect that Celia's finished "razoring" my hair, and as far as I can tell I'm not bald, although I haven't peeked yet. I'm actually feeling somewhat relaxed now. I can tell she's doing something else to my hair, but I don't care. Then I feel something wet, and I open an eye and look into the mirror to see that my head looks like something from an old sci-fi movie. There are silver pieces of aluminum foil sticking out in every direction. I shut my eyes again and block this scene from my mind, vaguely wondering if hats are in fashion this summer.

"Do you want a magazine?" asks Celia after a bit. "For while you wait?"

"I can fit Hannah in for quick manicure," calls a petite Asian woman from across the room. "Lori asked if I had time."

"Great," says Celia. "Can you keep it to twenty minutes or less?"

The woman nods as she hurries over and takes me by the hand and leads me to another station, where thankfully there is no mirror for me to gape at.

"Lori is good customer," she tells me as I sit in the chair at a table. "She told me take care of you." Then she smiles. "I am Lan."

I nod, remembering the name. "I've heard you're very good."

She looks down as if she's embarrassed. "I do my best."

The next thing I know she is soaking my hands in warm, soapy water, and it actually feels rather nice. "Lori says give you French manicure," she informs me as she begins working on one hand.

I just shrug. Why should I argue since everything seems settled anyway? Even so, I try to imagine what my mates back home would think if they could see me sitting here. Would they laugh at me? Or would they be impressed and wish that they were being treated so well? Sophie would probably enjoy all this pampering. She tries to act tough, probably for my sake, but I reckon she could get into this. Anyway, I tell myself, it should be good entertainment some evening when we're bored and wishing we had a telly. I'm good at storytelling, and I reckon I can embellish this one enough to create something quite amusing.

"Time to check your hair," says Celia.

"Let those nails air dry," instructs Lan. "Very pretty, yes?"

I look down at my unexpectedly natural-looking nails. They are soft pink and glossy with white tips. "Yes," I tell her. "Very pretty. Thank you."

"Thank you," she calls as Celia leads me back to her station.

Now seems to be the moment of truth, and despite my earlier bravado, I no longer feel at ease. "I can't bear to look," I admit as Celia removes a piece of foil.

"Just right," she says. Then she quickly removes the other pieces of foil, and the next thing I know we are back at the washing station again. My hair will be really clean by the time we leave this place.

Finally she is finished rinsing and conditioning and towel dry-ing and whatnot, so she leads me back to her station where I stare at my image in the mirror.

"What do you think?"

"I—uh—I don't quite know."

Aunt Lori is standing behind me now. I can see her smile in the mirror. "I think it's going to be just perfect."

I notice my expression in the mirror, and I try not to seem so stunned. But I just sit there staring, not knowing what to think. The color isn't as shocking as I had prepared myself for. But the cut makes it look like my hair is sticking up all over, and I'm certain it will never go into a ponytail again.

"Let's get it dried," says Celia.

I decide to shut my eyes again as the blow dryer begins buzzing about like a giant pesky insect. I will pretend that none of this is actually happening, that it's just a dream. A very weird dream.

"There now," says Celia. "How's that?"

I cautiously open my eyes again, and now the color is actually brighter than before, but at least my hair isn't sticking out in every direction. I study it carefully and finally decide that it's not too bad.

"What do you think?" asks Aunt Lori.

I kind of shrug. "It's okay."

"Okay?" repeats Celia with disappointment. "It's fantastic."

"She's just not used to it," says my aunt. "Give her time."

"Speaking of time . . ."

"Yes," says Aunt Lori. "I know you're closing now. Put this on my bill, and of course, add the standard tips . . . and an extra 10 percent for squeezing us in like this."

Celia smiles. "Thanks, Lori. Glad we could be of help. If it wasn't after five, I'd run Hannah over to Gina and let her play with some makeup."

Aunt Lori waves her hand. "I've got that covered. Vanessa and I are going to have her try some things at home."

Well, that's news to me. As we go back out to Aunt Lori's car, I give my head a shake in the sunshine. To my surprise it feels pretty good. Then I run my fingers through my hair and realize that my hair feels pretty good too. Kind of light and free. "Maybe this won't be so bad," I say to Aunt Lori once we're in the car.

She turns and looks at me, then smiles. "You look beautiful, Hannah."

I think it's the first time anyone has ever told me that. I mutter a thank you, then turn and pretend to look at something out the window. *Beautiful?* Is that even possible? Or is she just being nice? Not that I ever worried about my looks before. I reckon I could've had it far worse. Like Grace Lemke back at the mission. She's the same age as me and a nice girl, but she's quite heavy, and her hair is so thin that you can see her scalp. And then there's Amy Stevens, whose skin is always covered with severe acne, even on her back and chest. I feel sorry for those girls and have just been thankful that I don't have worries like that. Even so, I've never considered myself beautiful. Now, I reckon Sophie is quite pretty with her dark, curly hair and fair skin and blue eyes. I might even think she's beautiful sometimes, like when she's all scrubbed up. But not me. Those two words—*beautiful* and *Hannah*—just do not belong together.

eight

IS IT POSSIBLE THAT I AM BECOMING VAIN? I'VE ALWAYS DISLIKED VANITY in people. It seems such a weakness of character to me. I remember one girl in particular who was in our group home when I was fifteen. Her name was Nicole Flynn, and she was a year older than me and, according to her, far more sophisticated than the rest of us. I'll admit she was rather pretty with her pale blonde hair and icy blue eyes—a very delicate kind of pretty. Like a fragile butterfly wing that I found in the bush one day. I wrapped it in a tissue and put it in my shirt pocket, but it was crushed by the time I got back to my room. Unfortunately, her beauty was also only skin-deep because she wasn't very nice—not to anyone. She seemed to think she was royalty and we were all just little peasant girls sent by the angels to serve her. She always hogged the bathroom, spreading her things all over the bench and taking the best mirror for herself, and she was rude to the other girls.

I decided then that if being pretty meant being mean, I wanted no part of it. But I did feel sorry for Nicole toward the end of her stay with us. She hadn't made a single friend among the girls. In fact, she had many enemies. And one of her enemies, a girl named Rena, got into Nicole's diary and read it out loud to the rest of us. Everyone laughed, including me, but in truth I thought it was pitiful. You could tell that Nicole was miserable and lonely and perhaps even on the edge. Then it all came to a swift end when she tried to kill herself. Her parents were called out of the bush, and they all went back home to Australia to sort things out. I remember feeling guilty at the time, thinking that if I'd been a bit more friendly to Nicole . . . But most of all, I think I was glad she was gone and that things could return to normal. And I promised myself that I would never become vain like that.

Now as I stand here in front of my mirror in the privacy of my room, with my fancy new haircut and hair color, sporting these expensive designer clothes and shoes and accessories, and even wearing a bit of makeup provided by Vanessa and Aunt Lori, well, I reckon I look pretty "hot," as Vanessa puts it. As I strut around my room, putting on airs just for the fun of it, I think I look like someone altogether different than the Hannah who arrived in the States a few weeks ago. It's actually quite amazing. Even Vanessa and Aunt Lori were amazed. And I can tell they won't be embarrassed to be seen with me now. I've already delegated my old bathers to the back of my closet. I did take the time to pack them in my port and zip it up, zipping away the old Hannah with them.

Not that I have changed on the inside. And I certainly won't become like Nicole Flynn. But a little exterior change couldn't hurt anything. In fact, I think it could improve me in many ways. Like Aunt Lori says, "How you look reflects how you see yourself, and others will see it too." Or as Vanessa puts it, "Dress for the life you want to have." Although I'm not sure what that means.

Finally, after I've tried on every possible outfit, mixing and matching pieces and changing accessories the way Aunt Lori has shown me, I carefully hang everything up in my closet. I stand there for a moment, amazed at the wardrobe I've amassed in just two days.

It's far more clothes than I usually have at one time—at least new. The funny thing is that Vanessa was feeling sorry for me. "Your closet is so bare," she said after we played with makeup tonight. "You really need to do some more shopping." Naturally, I just laughed and told her that I've done more shopping in the past three days than I have in my entire lifetime. Of course, she didn't think that was possible, but I honestly don't think it was too much of an exaggeration.

I decide to pick out my work outfit for the morning since I have to be up so early. Despite Aunt Lori's and Vanessa's opinions of the clothes I bought at Ross, I'm hoping I can integrate them with some of the nicer items. That way I'll look stylish at work but still have more clothes to choose from. Finally I decide on the khaki skirt from Ross and the pale green Versace jacket that Aunt Lori insisted was a "must." I choose a white T-shirt (one of the cheapies) to go underneath the costly jacket, then select a bright, multicolored belt by Prada "to accent," as Aunt Lori says. And I think it works. To be practical, I decide to go with my inexpensive sandals. Then, just for fun, I try the mules instead, and although I don't really understand fashion, I think they work just fine. If not, I'm sure I'll hear about it, although it's a relief to know that neither Aunt Lori nor Vanessa will be up when I go to work early in the morning.

Uncle Ron has given me a map marked with several routes for getting to work. "But you can follow me tomorrow," he told me tonight. "Just to be safe. I'll take you on what's normally the quickest route. The traffic's not too bad that early in the morning, but just thirty minutes later it can be all locked up." Then he looked up from his desk and seemed to notice something. "Did you change your hair, Hannah?"

I kind of grinned. "Yeah. It was Aunt Lori's idea."

He nodded. "Looks nice."

"I'm getting used to it."

"You think your parents will mind?"

I considered this. "They've always encouraged me to be independent," I began. "But girls aren't allowed to use hair dye at school. I reckon they'll say it's my hair and my worries to sort out later."

He laughed. "I guess that's a pretty good attitude."

"See you in the morning."

"Bright and early."

And so I've got all my new clothes laid out, and I've washed my face the way Aunt Lori told me to. "You have to take better care of your skin," she warned me. "Especially when you're using makeup. You have to properly remove it and then apply a little nighttime moisturizer, and you should use UV protection during the day." She gave me all sorts of things, and I'm afraid I won't even remember what some of them are for, but I can go back for a refresher course later.

I'm all ready for bed now, and I'm feeling excited about starting my new job tomorrow. The alarm is set, and I know I should turn off the light. But I'm not quite ready to sleep, and I can't quite figure out why. I sit there for several minutes and finally it hits me. In the past when something new and exciting was going to occur the following day, I would spend a fair amount of time reading my Bible and then praying. I would ask God to help and guide me, and then I would peacefully go to sleep.

I actually consider doing this tonight, but then I feel slightly hypocritical. As if I've been going off on my merry way and suddenly I'm getting nervous, so I come to God and expect him to just forget the fact that I've totally ignored him for so long. It seems wrong. Even selfish. Perhaps if I'd brought my Bible with me, I wouldn't feel so bad opening it up and reading it. But since it's not here, I really can't do much about that. And so I turn off the light and lie down and try not to feel too anxious about how my new job will go in the morning.

I reckon I tossed and turned half the night, and the next thing I know, my alarm is going off. Even so, it is a relief to get up. For some reason this day is looming before me like a huge history exam, and I just want to get through it and move on. I dress carefully, taking time to put on my makeup just the way Vanessa and Aunt Lori instructed. I'm sure it doesn't look as good as when they did it, but perhaps it'll improve with time. Finally I give myself one last glance in the mirror, and I reckon I look pretty good. I'm not entirely sure about my orange purse, but it does seem to make the belt pop out a bit. Then I remind myself that I'm only going to work, not to some fancy party with Vanessa's fashion-conscious mates.

Uncle Ron is just finishing his coffee when I come down. "Want some joe?" he asks, holding up a cup.

"Joe?"

"Coffee. There's time if you want some, or breakfast—"

"No," I tell him. "I'm too nervous to eat right now. Maybe I can grab something later. I assume I get a break or something."

He laughs. "Yes. We don't chain you to the desk. And there's a coffee shop just down the street, as well as several kiosks. You'll be fine."

"Good."

"And you look very nice," he says. "Just right for work."

I nod. "Good. I was hoping—"

"Okay, then, just keep your map handy and follow me." He pauses as if just thinking of something. "You know, we'll have to get you a cell phone, Hannah."

"Oh, no," I say quickly. "I don't really need—"

"No, you *do* need one. Just in case you have engine trouble or get lost. I'll make sure that you have one by the end of the day."

So I thank him, and we go out; then I follow him as we head toward the freeway. It's helpful having him lead like this since it reminds me to stay on the right side of the road. And I make mental notes of things we pass and signs and whatnot. It actually seems rather simple. And although the traffic moves fast on the freeway, I am surprised at how at ease I am while following Uncle Ron. We exit this freeway and get onto another, and after about fifteen minutes, we are downtown where the buildings loom high above us. I follow him down into what seems to be a dark hole but actually turns out to be underground parking. He parks in a spot marked with his name and indicates that I'm to park in the one next to it.

"You get some special privileges being the niece of the owner," he explains when I get out. "Plus, that's my Jeep and I don't want it getting dinged."

He leads me to a lift and talks as we go up. "I'll introduce you to your manager first thing. She's a nice lady by the name of Cynthia Archer."

"Do I call her Mrs. Archer?" I ask. "Or Ms. Archer?"

"Just Cynthia."

I nod, taking this in. Yanks are so casual about some things and rather uptight about others. For instance, they call superiors by first names but items of clothing by last names. It's all rather convoluted, if you ask me.

But Cynthia turns out to be rather sweet. She shows me around and even lets me get a coffee before putting me to work at the desk that is situated at the main entrance.

"It's pretty simple," she says as she shows me how to work the phone lines and the computer. "I know it might seem complicated at first, but trust me, it gets easier. Mostly you're like traffic control. You just greet people and direct them along their way."

I take notes and ask questions. She walks me through a few phone calls, and I'm thinking maybe it's not so complicated after all.

"You ready to try it on your own?"

"I reckon." I smile what I hope looks like a confident smile. "But can I ring you if I need help?"

She nods. "By all means." And I assume that means yes.

"Alright, then. I think I'm good to go."

And at first I'm doing just fine. But suddenly, too many things are happening at once. First I get a call that's a complaint about one of our janitors who apparently left the water running and flooded a break room. And I'm not even sure what a break room is, but then another line lights up and then another, and I don't quite know what to do. Cynthia said not to put anyone on hold if I can help it. But I can't seem to help it. "Johnson's Janitorial," I say again and again. "May I put you on hold?" And without giving them a chance to respond, I hit the button. But I also accidentally cut someone off, and I have no idea how to get him back.

"I want someone over here immediately," the angry man is saying to me, and I remember this is the flood situation.

"I will get someone right on it, sir," I assure him. "I'm terribly sorry, and I know that we'll do whatever is necessary to straighten this out."

"Are you from Australia?" he asks, his tone becoming friendlier.

"Actually Papua New Guinea," I tell him, knowing that I'm probably wasting precious time, but then this man is the one with the flooding dilemma.

"Papua New Guinea? I've always wanted to go there. I spent some time in Australia and wanted to get up there but just couldn't—"

"Sir?" I interrupt. "Wouldn't you like me to get someone to come clean up your flooding situation?"

"Yes," he says quickly. "Of course."

"I'll get right on it."

"Thank you."

And so I need to get Cynthia back to find out what needs to be done for the flood situation, as well as try to answer the ongoing calls and retrieve the ones who've been stuck on hold. And suddenly I'm worried that I might be sweating and spoiling my new Versace jacket. I wish I'd thought to use antiperspirant like Vanessa had suggested.

"Just take it easy," Cynthia is telling me.

"Right," I say as I stand up and remove my jacket and hang it on the back of my chair. "Take it easy."

"Nice jacket," she says.

"Thanks."

"Let me walk you through this one more time." Then she sits down next to me, and together we take calls and work things out, and I am so relieved to have her help. It reminds me of how I felt while following Uncle Ron through the maze of freeways this morning.

By midmorning I am feeling a bit more confident. And I actually find some antiperspirant in the WC, which I really should call the ladies' bathroom, along with hairspray and lotion and mouthwash, which I assume are for anyone to use. I've never seen anything like it before, but then these Yanks seem to think of everything.

Cynthia gives me some employee paperwork to fill out and tells me that my lunch break starts at eleven and is one hour long. "We stagger the lunch breaks so that the phones are always managed. Some go at eleven and some at noon."

"Eleven's good for me," I say. "Especially since I get off at two."

"I noticed you didn't bring a lunch."

"I never even thought about that," I admit.

"No problem. There are several places to choose from." Then she writes down some names with fairly simple directions.

"I don't know what I'll do with a whole hour," I say as we both head to the time clock that keeps track of when you are or are not working.

"Some people walk for exercise. Some go shopping. Some bring books to read. And some just sit around and gossip. I'd invite you to join me for lunch today, but I need to run some errands."

"No worries," I tell her. "I'm sure I can find something to do."

She smiles. "And I'm sure you'll find that an hour goes by pretty fast."

"That's for sure," says a young woman named Carlita as she punches her card. "We're sharing a cab to Macy's Plaza today, if anyone else wants to come along."

"But we gotta hurry," says her friend, whose name I can't remember. "There's a big sale at Macy's—today only."

And I have no idea why, but the next thing I know, I am getting into a cab with Carlita and, as it turns out, Laticia. Within what feels like only seconds, we are there. "We could've walked," I say as we climb out of the cab that cost $10.

"Waste of time," says Laticia as she hands the driver a ten.

Carlita hands him a dollar that I think is for the tip. "We'll let you off easy since you're new. You can just pay $3."

So I dig in my purse for the money as we go into a large building that turns out to be a shopping center. But I can tell by the sign that there are food places nearby, and I reckon I'll be able to find something to eat here.

"Don't you want to hit Macy's first?" asks Carlita when she notices me starting to follow my nose toward the smell of food.

"Well, I thought I'd grab a bite—"

"You can do *that* later," says Laticia as she pulls me along with them. "Nice jacket," she says as she fingers the fabric of my sleeve. "Feels expensive."

"My aunt bought it for me."

"Must be nice," says Carlita. "Having rich relatives."

"I reckon," I say as we go into the department store.

nine

AFTER THAT, I AM SWEPT ALONG WITH THESE TWO. THEIR STYLE OF shopping is very different from anything I've experienced so far. It's more like a whirlwind, get-the-best-designer-for-the-lowest-price sort of shopping. Finally I decide that if you crossed my shopping spree at Ross Dress for Less with the way my aunt and cousin search out the best designers at the fancy shops, you might wind up with something like Carlita and Laticia's style of shopping. But I'm actually impressed with some of the things they are finding—as well as the prices.

"Wow," I say when I see the cute skirt that Carlita has found marked down to only $39. "I could almost afford something like that."

Carlita laughs. "Judging by the threads you're wearing, I'm sure you, or your aunt, could afford way more."

"Threads?"

"That jacket."

"Oh, right," I look down at my jacket. "Well, my aunt might be able to afford this, but I could never buy a Versace on my own."

"*Versace?*" Laticia pauses from flipping through a rack and looks at me with raised brows. "That's a Versace?"

I shrug. "Does the name really matter?"

"It would to me." Then she laughs. "Not that I'll ever have *that* problem. Although I did find a nice pair of Prada shoes at the thrift store last weekend. They'd hardly been worn at all."

"What's a thrift store?" I ask and am then treated to some of the secrets of dressing like a million when you have to work for a living.

Now Laticia holds up a green T-shirt. "This would go great with your *Versace* jacket, Hannah." She annunciates the name as if she wants to impress the lady in the next aisle. "Even if it's only a deek-nee."

"What's a deek-nee?"

"DKNY, or Donna Karon New York. Not exactly Versace but not half-bad either."

"It does go with my jacket," I admit as I examine the T-shirt. "But I'm a bit low on funds until payday."

"Get a credit card," says Laticia lightly.

"You mean a *charge account*?" I ask.

She laughs. "It's not as if I'm suggesting you get a tattoo."

"But a charge account? I'm only seventeen."

"Lots of girls your age have credit cards," says Carlita. "And I'm sure with your aunt as a cosigner you could easily get one too."

"And then you could capitalize on all these fantastic sales," continues Laticia as she holds a pair of bright yellow Capri pants up to her waist. "Just don't forget to pay the bill when your check comes. Otherwise you'll end up in deep—"

"Like you did?" says Carlita, pointing a finger at her friend. And then the two of them are going on about which one of them is more financially responsible. But their words float past me as I consider their suggestion.

A charge account? I'm thinking maybe that's not such a bad idea after all. At least I'm working now and making a decent wage, as it turns out. I was actually quite surprised when I learned how much I would earn per hour at Johnson's Janitorial. Far more than I'd imagined. I reckon I'll be set by the end of the summer. And I could probably afford to buy a few more things to round out my wardrobe in the meantime.

"Hey," says Laticia as she holds up the green T-shirt. "Why don't I just put this on my account, and you can just pay me back later." She winks at me. "I'm sure that you're good for it."

"Oh, no, I couldn't do—"

"No problem," she says. "It's perfect with that jacket. Way better than that boring white T-shirt you have on. I insist."

"But I can't—"

"Look," says Carlita, pointing toward the back of the store. "Why don't you just take the shirt back there to where it says accounts and tell them you'd like to open one. Fill out the paperwork and see what happens."

So I carry the T-shirt, which is steadily growing on me, to the counter, and I do as Carlita has instructed. I fill out the form as best I can, then hand it back to the woman. She glances over it and then asks if I have any major credit cards.

"No," I tell her, realizing this is probably just a foolish waste of time when I could be getting something good to eat instead. "I'm only seventeen," I say quickly. "And I just came to the States and am staying with my aunt and uncle, and this is probably not a—"

"Can one of them cosign for you?"

"Well, I'm not sure—"

"Is that their phone number?" She points to a line on the application.

"Well, yes, but I don't—"

"Hold on, honey." And the next thing I know she is dialing what I suspect is my aunt's phone number, and I am feeling extremely nervous. In fact, I am considering walking away and acting as if none of this ever happened, but then she already has my name and information and, it now sounds like, Aunt Lori on the phone.

"Very good," she's saying as she writes something down. "Yes, I agree completely, Mrs. Johnson. It's an excellent way for young people to begin learning about credit. Thank you very much." Now she turns to me with a bright smile. "Your aunt has cosigned, and you now have your own Macy's account with a credit balance of $2,000."

"*$2,000?*" I repeat in disbelief.

"I know that may seem conservative to start with. But you can always increase it over time."

"No no, it's just fine."

She does some things with her computer, then hands me a slip of paper with some numbers on it. "This will work until you get your regular card. It should arrive within the next week or so."

I glance at my watch to see that my lunch hour is half over and I still haven't had a bite to eat yet. But I do have a charge account now. Amazing.

Carlita and Laticia are loaded up with clothes and are just heading for the change rooms when I get back. "I thought this would look nice on you," says Laticia as she hands me a sleeveless top in a bright shade of turquoise. "It would look great with your hair and it's only $27, marked down from $89. Can you believe it?"

So I follow them into the change rooms, then try on the two tops and decide that both of them will be assets to my wardrobe. And as we're heading to the cashier, Carlita spots a rack of raincoats. "Oh, isn't this adorable?" she says as she holds up a lime-green trench coat. "Too small for me, but it would fit you, Hannah And this color would be fantastic on you. Here, try it on."

Suddenly I am standing in the middle of the store wearing a lime-green raincoat, and everyone is saying how totally great it looks on me. And as I look in the mirror, I can't disagree. But the price tag says that it's $250. Too rich for my blood.

"They just came in on Friday," says the salesgirl. "New for fall."

"But it's only June," I say, incredulous.

Laticia turns to Carlita. "Just wait until Hannah sees all the Christmas trappings in place by mid-October. Poor unsuspecting thing."

Carlita laughs, and I remove the raincoat, put it back, and step away as if the garment is armed and dangerous.

"The selection probably won't last for long," continues the salesgirl. "Already I'm out of the larger sizes in that same style."

"Do you have a raincoat?" asks Carlita.

"No, but it's so warm here that—"

"But we can have torrential downpours occasionally," says Laticia convincingly. "You really need a good raincoat, Hannah."

So by the time the salesclerk tallies up my purchases, with tax, I am in debt for more than $300. The surprising total makes me rather queasy, but then I remind myself that I will earn that much money in just a few days, and I feel a tiny bit better. Even so, I'm nervous as I sign my name in the funny little box that reminds me of the Etch A Sketch I had as a child. But I feel something else inside me too. It's this mixture of giddiness and excitement. And as the woman hands me my crisp Macy's bag and says, "Have a nice day," I'm thinking that shopping is actually rather thrilling.

"We just have time to grab hot dogs," says Carlita as she glances at her watch. Then, like a military commander, she says, "I'll finish up my purchase here. Hannah, you run outside and get us a cab. Laticia, you go pick up some hot dogs, and we'll all meet in front and eat in the cab."

"Right," says Laticia, then asks me what I want on my hot dog.

"Just mustard," I tell her. "No tomato sauce."

"Huh?" she looks confused.

"Ketchup," I mean, realizing my mistake. "No ketchup."

Then, following Carlita's instructions, I run out and flag down a cab, and within three minutes we're piled into the back, packages heaped around us. We wolf down our dogs just in time to be dropped off at the office.

"That was fun," I tell them as we hurry to the time clock. "Thanks for letting me tag along."

"Anytime," says Carlita as she punches her card and turns to face me. "You've got mustard on your chin, Hannah."

Laticia calls out, "Later!" as she heads back to her cubicle. I punch my time card, stow my Macy's bag, and return to my desk at exactly noon.

The rest of the day passes fairly uneventfully, and I only have to call on Cynthia for help a couple more times. "You're really getting the hang of it," she tells me. "I think you'll be an old pro by the end of the week."

"I hope so."

"Oh, your uncle sent this down." She reaches into her pocket to retrieve a sleek, silver cell phone. The kind that flips open and has a screen on it.

"Wow," I say, impressed. "I don't even know how to use it." So she gives me a basic lesson, and it doesn't seem too complicated.

"I don't really have anyone to call," I admit.

"That's okay," she assures me. "In my opinion they should mainly be used for emergencies. I get so irritated when I hear people using them in restaurants or theaters. So rude."

"I know what you mean."

Finally the day ends, and it's time to go home. But as I pick up my Macy's bag, I feel surprisingly tempted to return to that store. And not to see if I can return these items but because I'm wondering what other things I may have missed. What if there are more great things that I could get "on sale"? Carlita said it was a "one-day-only sale," and we had such a short amount of time to look. Finally I tell myself that I'm acting like a complete idiot and that I should just get into Uncle Ron's Jeep and go directly home. But even as I'm navigating my way back home, retracing my morning route, I think I recall seeing the name *Macy's* at one of the other malls, maybe the one that Aunt Lori took me to. I'm not sure. But maybe I should go and check it out to see if my magic number buys me instant credit with the other stores too.

"Don't be such a silly fool!" I chastise myself out loud as I cautiously enter the freeway, then speed up to stay with the traffic. "Focus on your driving and get home in one piece!"

Fortunately I do. And by the time I park the Jeep in the garage and push the button to close the door, I realize that I'm actually rather exhausted. I retrieve my bag from the passenger's seat and go inside. To my relief, the house is quiet, and no one seems to be about. I'm not sure why, but I'm not overly anxious for Aunt Lori or Vanessa to see that I've been out shopping today. Perhaps it's my pride. Am I embarrassed because I made such a fuss over being forced to shop in the past but today did it on my own free will? Or maybe I'm still a bit uncomfortable with the whole charge-account thing. Whatever it is, I'm glad no one's around.

And I feel rather stealthy as I sneak up to my room and quietly unload my new clothes. I remove the tags and hang them, one by one, in my closet, then step back to admire everything. This looks like the wardrobe of someone fairly impressive. Or at least not Hannah Johnson, MK from PNG.

Then I step back and scrutinize my image in the mirror again. I'm still getting used to this new look. But I'm definitely liking it. I can't help but wonder what someone like Wyatt or even that snooty Felicia would think of me now.

After a short but refreshing nap, I slip into my bikini and head down to the pool. But once I'm outside, I can hear voices.

"Hey, Hannah," calls Vanessa. "I thought you should be home by now. How's the working girl?"

I walk over to where she and Elisa are stretched out in lounge chairs, soaking up the sun and drinking iced tea. "Work wasn't so bad," I tell her as I stand there, careful not to cast a shadow over them.

Elisa lifts her sunglasses and squints up at me. "Hey, I like your hair, Hannah. Very cool."

"Thanks."

"Pull up a chair," says Vanessa. "There's enough sun to go around."

"Right." I set my towel aside and pull a lounge chair next to Vanessa's.

"Seriously," she says as she leans back, "you like working for Dad?"

"Yeah. It was okay, actually. The day went by pretty fast, and I even got to go shopping on my lunch break." Now I can't believe I admitted this, but it's too late to take it back. I arrange my towel on the chaise and lie down.

"*You* went shopping?" Disbelief fills Vanessa's voice. "Without anyone holding a gun to your head?"

"Amazing, isn't it?"

"What did you get?" asks Elisa.

So I tell them about the sale at Macy's and how I got "a couple tops and a raincoat," but I don't think they're overly impressed.

"Who's the raincoat by?" asks Elisa in a sleepy tone.

"Via something," I say, trying to remember the exact name.

"Via Spiga?" asks Vanessa.

"Yeah, that's it."

"Hmm . . ." murmurs Elisa. "Might not be too bad." Then she turns over to sun her back.

"It's lime green," I tell them, suddenly feeling hopeful.

"Sounds nice," says Vanessa. "You'll have to show me."

Suddenly, and inexplicably, I get up. "I'm going to get some iced tea," I tell them, knowing that I have something else in mind as well. And when I return with my tea, I am wearing my new raincoat over my bikini. And before I know it, I am strutting back and forth across the pool deck like I'm in a fashion show. And they are laughing and then hooting as I open the coat to reveal the plaid lining, as well as my bikini, underneath.

"Nice outfit," says Elisa. ."Perfect for that rainy day at the beach."

"Or for riding the big one," adds Vanessa.

Then I set my new Via Spiga raincoat almost reverently on a table that's in the shade, safe from any pool splashes, and rejoin them. I feel, for the first time since I arrived in the States, like I almost fit in.

ten

MY PARENTS ARE IMPRESSED WHEN THEY RING ME TOWARD THE END of the week. "You already got a job!" exclaims my mom. "How industrious."

"Yeah," I tell her. "And it's really great. I can save up all kinds of money by the end of the summer." My mom is relaying this information to my dad as I speak. I think they're in Texas today.

"Dad says that he hopes you take some time out for fun too. You know what they say about all work and no play."

"No worries," I assure them. "Vanessa makes sure that I get to play." Then I tell her about the beach party that we're going to on Saturday and how I may even rent a surfboard. "I just want to see if I can still do it."

"You be careful out there," warns my mom.

I laugh. "More careful than back in New Guinea?"

"Yes, well, you're probably right. Surfing in Southern California is probably much safer."

We talk a bit more, and I give them my cell phone number, just in case. Then Mom reminds me that they love me and that, as always, they pray for me and my brothers every single day.

"I love you guys too," I tell her, carefully omitting the praying daily thing. "You take it easy and don't work yourselves to death out there on the road."

"We won't. And same to you."

"No worries."

"Call us if you need anything, sweetie," she finally says. I promise to do that, and then we hang up.

Sometimes it amazes me that I've spent so little time actually living with my parents. At least in these last five years. Before that, I lived in the village with them and with my brothers too before they went off to the group home and mission school and eventually to uni in the States. But back when I was younger, I always had village friends to play with, and my mom taught everyone who wanted to learn at our little village school. Most of the time I went barefoot, and I often wore the same dress for several days in a row before my mom insisted on stripping it off me and throwing it into the laundry. The way my mom did her washing was with this ancient wringer washer that was powered by petrol. When I was old enough, she even let me help but always warned me to keep my long hair pulled back so that it wouldn't get caught up in the wringers. These memories now seem like some scene from an old movie—or maybe just a dream. They're so vastly different and removed from the way I'm living these days. Sometimes I wonder which is real.

I finally checked my e-mail during break time at work. Cynthia said it's okay as long as it's not on company time. As I suspected, I had several messages from Sophie. The first few filled me in on the latest happenings at school. It's strange to think it's still the school year for them over there. How quickly I slipped into the whole "summer vacation" thing here. I'm glad I did the extra work earlier this year, allowing me to have this time off now. Hopefully I won't be too far behind when I return.

"You're so lucky to be out of school these days," her first e-mail says. "Mr. Fenwick is so brokenhearted by Miss O'Brien's rejection of his affections that he's taking it all out on us." And on she goes lamenting the usual troubles of the group home and secondary school and the disagreements between mates and mission life in general. But toward the end, she cheers up and reminds me that she's praying for me and that God loves me and then says, "I hope you've located a new Bible by now and that you're reading it again." Her next e-mails become briefer and I can tell that she's feeling sour that I haven't written back.

"I'm sure you're quite busy over there," she says. "Too busy to stay in touch with your old mate?"

Her guilt trip works, and I find myself writing back to her. I try to keep it brief and to the point. I tell her about my job and how fancy Vanessa's home is and how fast-paced life is here. But I don't say anything very personal. I'm not even sure why, but I suspect it has to do with the whole God thing. It's as if Sophie is this constant reminder to me that I'm not doing what I should be doing in the spiritual sense. As in not reading my Bible, praying, or going to church. I consider the fact that the mission school has "devotions" every day and how we get demerits for missing or even being late. And then there's the weekly Bible study and church on Wednesdays and Sundays. It's as if they live and breathe all this stuff on a continual basis. And it's unthinkable to take a break of any kind. It's funny how this seems like a completely foreign culture to me now. Almost as if all my old friends are living in a cult or something. And sometimes I wonder if I'll ever want to go back. And I guess that scares me a little.

"So as you can see, my life is really busy, and sometimes it's hard to take the time to check e-mail. So please don't feel bad if I don't get back to you right away. Remember what they say: No news is good news. So if you don't hear from me, you can just assume that everything's going great. . . ." I feel like such a phony as I hit the Send button. Not only that, but I feel like I'm starting to be a pretty bad excuse for a mate. But, I assure myself, I can work these things out later.

"Coming shopping with us today?" asks Laticia as she hurries past my desk with several packages of copy paper in her hands.

"Again?" I ask.

"It's Super Friday," she calls over her shoulder. "Customers with accounts get an additional 10 percent off almost everything."

"Ten percent?"

"You in?"

As it turns out, I *am* in. And once again the three of us leap into a taxi. I pay four dollars to cover my fair share, and within three minutes we're at the mall again. And this time I don't need any encouragement to skip food and go directly to Macy's. In fact, I don't even feel hungry as I make my way to the beachwear department. We've already agreed to meet around 11:50 to grab hot dogs and a cab. But all I can think is that now I can get something new and cool to wear to the beach party tomorrow. Vanessa told me, after I discreetly asked, that Wyatt Conners would *probably* be there.

"But I think he and Felicia are hooking up," she told me when we went out for Frappuccinos last night. "Elisa said they went sailing last weekend and that Felicia has her sights firmly set on him." Vanessa attempted a laugh. "And we all know that whatever Felicia wants, Felicia gets."

"How's that?" I asked, stupidly, of course.

Vanessa just looked at me with those wide, blue eyes, still

thinking, I'm sure, that I'm the biggest lamebrain in Orange County. "Felicia's dad is loaded."

"So is yours," I reminded her. "But what's that got to do with anything?"

"In the first place, my dad is *not* loaded. Not like Felicia's dad anyway. Felicia's dad inherited money and businesses, and he's worth like millions, maybe billions, I don't know for sure. But I've heard he owns businesses all over the world. And they have like six or seven homes. Felicia can basically have anything she wants."

"Meaning Wyatt?"

"This is the deal with Wyatt, Hannah: His parents were always pretty well off, okay? But they split up a couple years ago. And Wyatt lives with his mom, who's still trying to get an alimony settlement from his dad since he's the one with the actual money. Unfortunately, it's not going too well, and Wyatt's not able to . . . enjoy all the things he's accustomed to. So I'm sure that having Felicia as a girlfriend must be pretty tempting to him."

"And she's not hard to look at," I added, as if that made me feel any better.

"You got it."

"Well, it's not like I was in love with him," I told her. "I just thought he was nice, and he mentioned surfing and—"

"Yeah, Wyatt totally loves to surf. He's like the surfer dude of the bunch of us. He's really good too. And I'm sure that doesn't hurt Felicia's chances with him a bit either."

"She surfs too?"

Vanessa actually laughed then. "Not hardly. But the VanHorns own a beach house in Laguna—that's where the party is tomorrow—and it's in a pretty good surfing spot. And since it's a private beach . . . well, it doesn't take a genius to figure it all out."

"Wyatt's after Felicia for her beach?"

"Yeah, right. That and everything else. You can't really blame him, can you? I mean, it's a pretty nice package."

I nodded as if I understood this completely. And maybe I do a little now that I'm getting acclimated to this whole Orange County way of life. And maybe I'd be just as tempted by a package like that too. Who knows? Even so, I've always been an extremely competitive person. Whether in sports or grades or getting the biggest laughs from my mates in school, I've always enjoyed a fair match. And so, as I make a beeline for the swimwear section, I feel that I'm on a mission. But within moments I am completely overwhelmed. I try to remember the bikinis that Elisa and Vanessa wear and wish I'd thought to ask about the designers, although I'm not sure those kinds of designers can be found at Macy's. To be honest, I don't think their suits look all that different from the one I got at Ross. I still have so much to learn.

"Can I help you?" asks a girl who seems to be about my age.

"Yeah, I hope so." Then I quickly explain that I want something that looks good but won't go flying off me if I'm surfing—or rather falling on my face as I attempt to surf.

"Tommy," she says.

"Huh?"

"Hilfiger."

"Oh, right." And then I follow her over to a section where the primary colors are red, white, and blue. "Very patriotic," I comment, and she smiles as she grabs several bathers. One is a one-piece with stripes. Another is a two-piece, but not a bikini. Finally we determine what size I am, and she loads me down with a small pile of suits. I quickly try them on, one after the other, and I try not to be too critical of my figure, which is probably not as nice as Felicia's.

The salesgirl is actually quite helpful. She brings other sizes and helps me decide which ones look best. And by the time I'm finished, I have purchased a blue and white "tankini," as she calls it, which will be perfect for surfing, as well as a regular bikini that actually looks hot on me, if I do say so myself. Not only that, but she's also helped me find a beach bag, thongs, a "cover-up," and a few other Tommy things that she reckons will be "essential" for tomorrow's beach party.

"Do you think this is too much Tommy?" I ask as she tallies up my purchases.

She smiles. "Not for you. I think you're a real Tommy girl."

"A *Tommy* girl?" I'm not sure I like the sound of this. Not only that, I'm not sure what Vanessa will think since I know she's not really into Tommy.

"Yeah. You seem the sporty type to me. And I think you should go with the style that most fits you and your lifestyle."

I nod, thinking this makes sense. But I'm still not convinced.

"Minus your 10 percent discount for using your credit card, it comes to $538.72," she tells me, and it's all I can do not to fall over.

I repeat the figure, and she just smiles and points to the Etch A Sketch thing that I'm supposed to sign.

"You saved more than $53," she says. "That's almost like getting the bikini for free."

Once again, I feel slightly giddy and light-headed, but I obediently sign my name and then thank her as she hands me two bags of Tommy things. I try not to think about what the new balance on my charge account might be as I hurry to the exit. And I remind myself that I'm making good money, even if I am spending it before it gets here.

"You're late," yells Carlita as she wildly waves to me from the curb.

"Sorry," I say, running toward them, my bags slapping into my legs as I go.

"It's okay," she says, letting me climb into the cab before her. "It's only a couple of minutes. We'll be fine."

"I got your hot dog," says Laticia, handing it to me once we're all settled. "Just mustard and no *tomato sauce*."

"Thanks." I laugh as I take it. Then, between bites, I tell them about my purchases.

"Were they on sale?" asks Laticia as we climb out of the cab.

"Just the extra 10 percent," I say as I pay her for the cab fare and hot dog.

"Wow," says Carlita. "That must've cost a bundle."

"It'll be worth it," I tell them. Then, as we head inside, I explain about the beach party and how hard it is for me to try to fit in with all these rich kids.

"But you're such a great kid," says Laticia. "They should like you for who you are, not how much you're spending on clothes."

I study these two as we ride the lift up. And while they're fashionable in their own way, I realize that they have absolutely no idea what it's like to compete in Vanessa's crowd.

Once again, I stow my bags, thank my office friends, punch my time card, and hurry back to my desk. The feeling of excitement—the thrill of shopping and finding such great things—stays with me almost until the end of my shift. But by then I'm just plain tired.

"Have a good weekend," Cynthia says after I punch out.

"Thanks," I tell her as I open my locker to retrieve my Macy's bags. "You too."

"Looks like you've done some serious shopping," she observes as I loop the handles over my arm and then pull out my purse.

I nod. "Yeah, I got some things for a beach party."

"On your Macy's card?"

"Yeah. Today was 10 percent off."

"Be careful, Hannah," she says in a serious voice.

I stop to study her for a moment, wondering what she means exactly. I think I even feel offended by this, though Cynthia's nice to me and all. What business is it of hers what I buy?

"Don't get yourself into too much debt," she continues. "It can be awfully hard to crawl out from under that."

"Well, I don't really plan on buying anything else," I assure her. "I think I'm pretty much set now."

"Good. You know, I've learned through the school of hard knocks that it really doesn't take a whole lot of clothes or even a lot of money to acquire a decent wardrobe—if you go about it right."

I notice her navy blazer, which might even have a designer label inside—maybe Ralph Lauren since I happen to know (from Vanessa) that Lauren leans more toward the older, more classic styles. Cynthia is wearing this over a crisp, white shirt with neatly pressed khaki-colored pants, and I take a moment to observe how her brown leather shoes match her belt and purse. As usual, she looks quite well dressed and actually rather classy. "You always look so nice, Cynthia."

She smiles now. "There are some simple tricks to it. Let me know if you ever want me to share them with you."

"Thanks," I tell her. "I'll keep that in mind."

But as I ride the lift down to the parking area, I'm not so sure that I want to dress like Cynthia. Oh, sure, she looks great, but then she's a lot older than me, and I rather enjoy the fun kinds of clothes that Vanessa and her mates wear. Even if I can't actually afford all the fancy designer names, I guess it's true that I don't mind trying to look the part. I pile my bags into the back of the Jeep, feeling rather excited about trying out my new Tommy bathers tomorrow. I'm imagining myself wearing the tankini and riding my rented board with both grace and style. Hey, it could happen.

As I drive toward home, I try not to consider Cynthia's warning about not getting in over my head in debt. I understand and even appreciate her concern, but really, I don't think that's going to happen to me. And like I told her, I reckon I'm all set for summer now. I really don't think there will be any more big shopping sprees in my future.

From here on out, I will try to save almost everything I earn. Maybe I'll even open a special account for it. I just wish that payday wasn't still a whole week away since I'm really getting low on cash. Not only that, but I realize that I still need enough money to rent a board tomorrow, and I have no idea how much that might cost.

I pull into the driveway and wonder if I should ask Uncle Ron for a draw on my salary. I overheard one of the janitors saying that he was getting a draw today so that he could take his wife out for their anniversary. And while I'm not looking for any special favors, I would think that being the niece of the owner should be worth something.

eleven

"LOOKS LIKE SOMEONE'S GONE SHOPPING AGAIN," SAYS VANESSA WHEN I'm barely through the door.

"Hi to you too," I retort, wishing I had left these bags in the car until later, like midnight.

"What did you go and do now?" she says in a slightly superior and teasing tone. "Another raincoat perhaps?"

I set the bags on the shiny countertop, just like I've seen her do before. "Not a raincoat," I tell her in a stiff voice. "Some beach things. I thought I might need a proper set of bathers if I'm gonna try to surf tomorrow. I don't really want the top of my bikini to come off if I take some horrific plunge."

"You're really going to surf?" she asks as she helps herself to a peek inside a bag.

"Why not?"

"Wow, it looks like you mugged Tommy Hilfiger."

"Right." Now, I thought I was prepared for this, but something about her tone is rather aggravating. "I decided that I should go with a style that suits me," I say, echoing the salesgirl's pitch.

She nods. "Yeah, I guess that makes sense." She holds up the top of the tankini. "This might actually look good on you. You've got that great long waist that can pull off a suit like this."

So then I'm tugging out all the other items, holding them up one by one and explaining why I got them and why I think they're totally cool. By the time I stop to take a breath, she looks a bit overwhelmed by my unbridled enthusiasm.

"Uh, that's a lot of Tommy stuff, Hannah."

I frown. "Do you think it's too much?"

But she just shrugs. "Not if you're okay with it. And it's not like you have a lot of other options anyway. To be honest, your other bikini is, hmm, how do I put this nicely? Well, it's like so *yesterday*."

"So *yesterday*?"

"Yeah. That's obviously why they had it at Ross. Everything there is like so yesterday. But, I'll give you this, that bikini is way better than that other excuse of a swimsuit you brought with you. Man, I hope you've burned that one by now."

"Yeah, sure," I lie. "I threw it away last week."

"That's a relief." She holds up the Tommy bikini now. Despite the minimal amount of fabric, it's got these rather large blocks of red and blue on it with a bit of white trim. Kind of clever, I thought. Plus it looked pretty cool on. Even the salesgirl was impressed.

"This is pretty cute," she admits. "I wouldn't wear it myself, but I can imagine it on you."

"So do I pass then?"

She considers this. "If you're happy, I'm happy."

I sigh in relief. "Well, I'm happy."

"Now do you want to see what I got today?"

"Sure," I tell her and we go up to her room where she shows me her new bikini, a pastel number which cost far more than mine. Then she slips on some very pretty sandals that I actually feel slightly lustful for. And then a pale pink cover-up that doesn't appear to cover much. But she seems thrilled with her selections. And so I compliment her on her choices and say that if I had her kind of money, I'd probably get something cooler than Tommy too.

"But I'm just a poor working missionary kid," I tell her. "I gotta stay within my means."

She laughs. "Well, you may not be a fashion diva yet, but you've certainly come up a few notches. And summer has barely begun." Then she goes to her closet and emerges with a pair of sunnies with large, dark blue frames. "These shades are Tommy Hilfiger," she tells me. "Why don't you take them since I never wear them anyway?"

"Cool." I try them on and check out my image in her big mirror. "Thanks a lot."

"Now we should go down and work on our tans," she suggests as she starts pulling off her top.

"Right," I say, dashing back to my room. "Meet ya down there." I dump out the contents of my bags all over my bed, a Yankee sea of red, white, and blue. I examine my treasures again, finally deciding to try out my new bikini today, just to make sure that my tan lines match it correctly. My stomach finally peeled, and fortunately the tan is starting to match up with the rest of me now. I put the new sunnies into the beach bag along with the Tommy thongs and cover-up, just to see if it all works, and suddenly I feel like I'm almost there. I'm almost in the same league as Vanessa and Elisa. Now, as far as Felicia goes . . . well, I don't really want to think about that yet. Maybe later when my head is clear and I'm feeling more relaxed.

After sunning with Vanessa for nearly an hour, I cannot take it anymore. I decide to dive into the pool. I swim a few laps, satisfied that my Tommy bikini holds up just fine for swimming. The top actually stayed in place during and after my dive, making me think it might actually work for surfing, once I determine how well I can stay upright on the board, that is. Finally I climb out and fall like a dripping-wet noodle into the chaise next to Vanessa. I am about to fall asleep when I hear the muffled ringing of a cell phone. Mine is still upstairs, and I leave it turned off most of the time anyway. Vanessa says a foul word, then fumbles through her bag until she finally locates it. Then, after a quick recovery, she says, "Hey," in her laid-back telephone voice. After a few seconds of silence she continues, this time with a bit more enthusiasm, as if this was a call she really wanted to take. "Yeah, that sounds great." Pause. "Uh-huh, seven is fine. See ya."

Then she hangs up and turns to me and lets out a high-pitched squeal that makes the yardman, who is working on a hedge past the pool, nearly jump out of his sneakers. "Do you know who that was?" she demands as if I'm clairvoyant or something.

"Who?"

"Only *Bryce Fisher.*"

"Oh . . ." I nod, recognizing this name. Bryce, I already know, is Vanessa's primary love interest of late. They started dating toward the end of the school year, going to the prom and then Bryce's graduation party. But practically the next day, Bryce was whisked off with his grandma on a trip to the Mediterranean, or some exotic place like that, apparently to keep her company since she was still getting over the loss of her husband.

"So he's back?"

"Yes!" she exclaims happily. "And he's taking me out tonight and plans to be at the beach party tomorrow." She sighs now. "Oh, life truly is beautiful, Hannah."

"It'll be fun to actually meet him," I tell her. I've seen his photos, and frankly, I am not that impressed by his dark, somber eyes and overly serious expression. Also, I don't get the weird haircut or dark-framed glasses, which, in my opinion, make him look like a dag. Of course, I'd never admit this to my smitten cousin. But I am curious as to what she sees in this guy. Well, other than money. She told me he drives a very expensive Porsche that his grandmother gave him for graduation, so his family is obviously quite wealthy.

"Oh, Hannah, I feel bad to leave you home all alone," she says suddenly. "I guess you could come with—"

"No way!"

She looks relieved. "Oh, good. You really don't mind being home by yourself, do you? Because I know Mom and Dad are going out tonight too, but maybe you could join them—"

"Really, I'm perfectly fine on my own. I'm totally wrecked from my first week of work and getting up at the crack of dawn, you know. I might even go to bed early. And I don't mind having a bit of rest before the big party tomorrow."

"You're such a sensible girl, Hannah. Guess it comes from growing up as a missionary kid, huh?"

I shrug, then turn over to sun my back. "Yeah, maybe so," I mutter, wishing this conversation would end. I think the truth is, I'm not overly fond of being considered "sensible" these days. And if I could do just what I liked, I'd probably be rich and free and able to go out tonight too. Oh, not as a third wheel with Vanessa and Bryce. But I wouldn't exactly mind a date with Wyatt. As if that's ever going to happen. But even if she's poor, a girl can dream.

Later that afternoon, Vanessa makes me sit on her bed and watch as she tries on outfit after designer outfit, piling her expensive rejects on the floor.

"What's up?" asks Aunt Lori, sticking her head in the door.

"I don't have a thing to wear," moans Vanessa with more drama than seems necessary.

"For what?" asks Aunt Lori as she gives me a little hello wave.

Then Vanessa explains about Bryce getting home and their unexpected date tonight and how she wants to look totally perfect. "I mean, it's been two weeks since I've seen him, and he's been off in Europe looking at girls who are probably totally chic and rich and—argh!" She collapses onto the bed beside me, and for a moment I think she's actually passed out.

Aunt Lori seems to consider her daughter's quandary as she picks up a pair of pale yellow, low-cut Capri pants and gives them a shake. "These look awfully good on you, Vanessa."

Vanessa suddenly comes to, sits up, and takes notice. "Yeah, but with what?"

"How about that white Iceberg top of mine? The one you're always drooling over."

"Seriously? Mom! You'd let me wear that?"

"What are mothers for?"

Vanessa leaps to her feet and gives her mom a big hug. "You're the best, Mom."

"How about you?" Aunt Lori turns her attention to me now. "What are you up to tonight, Hannah? Big date?"

I make a laughing sound. "No way. I plan to just veg out tonight. I'm beat from my big working week."

"Hey," calls Uncle Ron from the hallway. "Guys allowed in there?"

Vanessa, who has been clad in only her bra and underwear up until now, quickly pulls on the closest T-shirt and jeans and tells her dad to come in. "Join the party," she says as she flops down on the bed again. Then Aunt Lori fills him in on Vanessa's big plans and then, more pathetically, how I'm too worn out from all my hard work to go out and have any fun tonight.

"Wait," I say quickly. "I didn't mean it like that. I just don't really want to go out tonight. And besides, we're going to that beach party tomorrow, and I need to rest up so I can surf."

Uncle Ron chuckles. "Now that's something I'd like to see. Are you any good?"

I shrug. "It's been a while. But I used to have fun."

"What are you using for a board?"

"Guess I'll have to rent one." Of course, this reminds me of my hopes for getting a draw. As much as I hate to ask this in front of everyone, I'm not sure when I'll have this opportunity again. "Do you know how much that will cost? I'm running a bit short on cash . . . in fact, I was sort of wondering if I might possibly get a draw. I heard someone at work saying that he was getting a draw and I thought—"

"Of course!" Uncle Ron slaps his forehead with his palm. "I should've realized that you'd be running low on cash by now. Just let me go down to my office, and I'll write you a check." He glances at his watch. "And if you hurry, Hannah, you might even make it to the bank before closing time. There's a small branch of U.S. Bank right down the—"

"Right," I say quickly. "You mean the one in Stanley Square."

The next thing I know, I've got a check for $2,000 in my purse, and I'm driving Uncle Ron's Jeep over to the bank and opening an account.

"You're Ron Johnson's niece?" says the olive-skinned woman who's helping me. "He's one of our favorite customers."

"I'm staying with them," I explain. "And he's letting me work at his business for the summer."

"Isn't that nice." She's looking over the paperwork I filled out. "So you want checking and savings?"

"That's right. Mostly savings, I reckon. But Uncle Ron told me to get a checking account too. Although I've never written a check in my life."

She smiles. "You'll learn fast. And nowadays most people rarely write checks anyway." She goes on to explain how a debit card works. "You can use them anywhere. And we have ATMs all over."

"What's an ATM?" I ask.

Then she explains, and I realize that everything in the States seems to be invented for the purpose of saving time. And yet everyone seems to be running around as if there's not enough of it.

"Would you like to have it activated for Visa too?"

I frown. "But I'm actually a citizen," I tell her. "At least I am here in the States. It's only over in New Guinea where I need a visa."

She laughs, then pats my hand. "You're charming, dear. No, I mean for credit. We can activate the Visa account, and then you can use your card to withdraw money from your checking—as a debit—or you can use it as a credit account. For when you're running low on cash."

"I can do that?"

She smiles. "Well, I may have spoken too quickly, but I'm guessing that because you're Ron Johnson's niece, it shouldn't prove much of a problem. But since it's getting late and this is Friday, perhaps I'll just run the paperwork on Monday. That is, if you want the Visa account activated."

"Okay," I finally agree, thinking it might save me from having to ask my uncle for any more advances. "I guess that would be convenient."

"Oh, yes. It's very convenient."

And just like that, it's done. I walk out with some temporary paperwork, a fistful of cash, and the promise of receiving actual cards in the next couple of weeks. Only in America!

When I get back home (funny how I think of this place as home now), no one is here. I walk around the quiet house for a bit and then finally decide to forage for food. Despite the fact that my relatives have money, they always seem to be short on food. Vanessa says it's because she and her mom are watching their weight. But Uncle Ron is never very happy about it. As a result, he picks up his own "supplies." Early on, he let me know where he stashes them. "Don't tell Vanessa or Lori," he warned. "They'll either eat it or throw it out. But feel free to help yourself."

And so I do. Back at the group home, we seldom get things like this—"junk food," as Vanessa calls it. But during my short stay in the States, I've already developed an appreciation for things like Cheetos and Ding Dongs and Snickers bars. I'm not overly fond of fizzy drinks (or soda, as it's called). They're a bit sweet for my taste. Well, other than the lemony sorts. And unfortunately, my uncle's taste leans more to Dr Pepper and Pepsi (neither of which I can stand) or beer. Now, I suppose I am wondering about the beer. Naturally, any form of alcohol is forbidden at both the mission and the school. Consequently neither of my parents drink or ever has as far as I know. But Uncle Ron usually has at least one, if not several, beers in the course of an evening.

One of my friends back in PNG (a braggy sort of girl named Leah) told me that she drinks beer all the time when she's "back home in Melbourne." She even claims that her grandparents give it to her. And she tells everyone she likes it! Not only that, but once she graduates and leaves PNG to go to uni Down Under, she says she plans to drink all the time.

I guess Leah has made me curious as to why so many people drink it and think it's so great. I look in the fridge to see that there are probably at least a dozen bottles of beer in there. And I wonder if my uncle will notice if one goes missing. And even if he does, will he ever guess that MK Hannah is the culprit? Probably not. So I go for it. I grab a beer, then take my bag of Cheetos and a Ding Dong and go out by the pool.

As expected, the Cheetos and Ding Dong taste just fine, but when I pop open the beer and take a big, long swig (just like my uncle does), the same swig comes spewing right back out and all over the patio. Yuck! And yuck again! I don't see how anyone can drink this nasty stuff. It tastes foul and bitter, like something you might use to clean upholstery. I go back inside and pour the smelly beer down the sink, then rinse and stow the empty bottle in the bin where my uncle drops them. Then I fill a pitcher with water, add a bit of soap, and take it out to clean up my mess.

I feel a bit embarrassed to have sneaked and then wasted one of my uncle's beers. But somehow I think he would understand. Not that I plan on telling him.

I finally tire of loitering around the backyard and decide to go inside and see what's on the telly tonight. After flipping through hundreds of channels, I eventually find an old black-and-white movie that looks good, but after about an hour I get so sleepy that I flick off the big flat screen and trek upstairs to finish watching the movie in my room. I remain slightly fascinated by the fact that I have a real live telly built right into the armoire that's in my room—and that it gets all the same channels as the big-screen one downstairs. But then, I realize, there are tellies in most of the rooms in this house, including the kitchen and laundry room, and even my aunt and uncle's master bathroom has its own flat screen. It's mounted on the wall and situated to be viewed from the comfort of the oversized jet tub. Truly amazing.

But I can finally keep my eyes open no longer. I reach for the remote and turn it off. I can still see the flickering images of the black-and-white movie in the backs of my eyeballs. It was an old thirties flick—kind of a Cinderella story. Very predictable and rather put-you-to-sleep boring. And yet it captured my attention too. And I felt I could relate to the character, a young girl who gets pulled into the world of the rich and famous and yet never quite fits in, although I'm sure it all ended well for her.

As I'm drifting to sleep, I tell myself that I *can* fit in. That money isn't everything and that people *can* get to know me for who I am and perhaps even like me. Do I pretend that I haven't spent far more money than ever before on clothes? Clothes that are meant to impress others? Of course not. Call it denial or survival or even fatigue. But somehow I do not believe it is wrong. Or so I tell myself as I fall asleep.

twelve

MOST PEOPLE WOULD SLEEP IN ON THEIR FIRST DAY OFF, BUT NOT ME. I'm up early as usual, and I reckon Uncle Ron is pleased that I made coffee.

"Thanks," he says as he heads out for work. He still works Saturdays at the office, even though he probably doesn't have to. "Have fun surfing today."

"Yeah," I say. "Hope I don't look like a total dork out there."

He laughs. "Don't worry, Hannah. I bet you'll be just fine. You seem like the kind of girl who always lands on her feet." I desperately hope he's right.

I drive the Jeep with the top down so that I can stick the board in back (Uncle Ron's suggestion). Plus, Bryce wanted to pick up Vanessa (in his classic Porsche, no doubt). Vanessa told me that the car had belonged to his grandfather before he died and that Bryce's dad was mad as a cut snake when Grandma-ma gave it to Bryce for graduation (well, those weren't her exact words). Apparently the car's worth about $100,000! I can't believe that any car is worth that much. Never mind that an eighteen-year-old kid gets to drive around in it for free. I really don't like to whinge, but sometimes I reckon life's *not* fair.

Renting the board is easy enough, so at least the day starts out well. But as soon as I hit the beach, things start to go downhill fast.

"Oh, what a darling suit, Hannah," Felicia says as I come out onto her family's private beach lugging my less-than-impressive rental surfboard. "My little sister used to have one just like that, back when Tommy was all the rage."

"Right," I say to her, nodding as if her words don't hurt. "Nice place you have here, Felicia. Thanks for inviting me."

She shrugs. "It's okay for a beach party now and then. But mostly we don't use it much. Daddy keeps threatening to sell it."

"Sell it?" says Wyatt as he joins us. "Hey, Hannah." Then his attention diverts back to Felicia. "Seriously, Felice, he's not going to sell this place, is he? You guys got one of the coolest spots down here."

She smiles, flirtatiously I think. "Maybe you should talk directly to Daddy, Wyatt. He seems to think you've got good sense. Especially after the way you saved our skin last weekend." Then she begins to recap their exciting adventure on the high seas, sailing about in her daddy's sixty-foot sailboat, higher than—

"Are Vanessa and Bryce here yet?" I ask, interrupting her tale.

"Over there." She points to some beach chairs and low tables that are arranged down in the sand near what appears to be a volleyball net.

"Thanks," I tell her with a smile about as genuine as her cup size. Vanessa already told me that Felicia had them "enhanced" for Christmas last year. Wonder how her parents wrapped that little present?

I trudge through the sand over to where Vanessa and Bryce are sitting and visiting with some friends. It has not escaped my attention that some of these kids, including Bryce, are consuming alcohol. Mostly beer it seems—the expensive kind with fancy labels. I'm not entirely sure what's in Vanessa's plastic cup. It looks pink and bubbly. Maybe just some fruity sort of soda.

"Hi," I say to Vanessa in a flat-sounding voice. Already I wish that I hadn't come. It's obvious that I am still the misfit in this crowd, Tommy Hilfiger or not. Sometimes I reckon I'm just a "glutton for punishment," as Sophie used to say.

"Oh, Hannah," Vanessa says sweetly. "I was just telling Bryce about you." Then she introduces me to him and her other mates, acting as if I am visiting royalty or a Down-Under celeb-type, perhaps a second cousin of Nicole Kidman or even Russell Crowe.

"Pleasure to meet you," I tell them.

"Don't you just *love* her accent?" says a girl named Bree. "Do you say *good day* too?"

I sort of roll my eyes, then give it to her correctly. "G'day, mates." This seems to amuse them, and I wonder if they're always this easy to please or if they're simply blotto.

"You're a surfer?" asks a sandy-haired guy. I think his name is Clayton, and I have to admit he's cute.

"I haven't been for quite a while," I confess. "But I thought I'd give it a shot today. Reckon I can't make too much of a fool of myself." I nod down to my tankini, which is solidly in place and probably has far more fabric than what all the other girls are wearing put together. "At least I should be able to keep my top on out there."

This makes them laugh and makes me feel a bit more at ease.

"Where's the rest of your stuff?" asks Vanessa.

"Still in the Jeep."

"Well, bring it down here and join us," she commands. "We're trying to get up a volleyball team for later on, and we want you on our side."

So I plop my board down and trudge back to the Jeep to retrieve the rest of my beach things. I feel a bit self-conscious as I pass by Felicia again, afraid she might announce how her little sister also has the rest of the Tommy stuff that I'm sporting today. But thankfully she seems fairly occupied with Wyatt and another guy, and I make it past them without any new jabs.

"What are you drinking, Hannah?" Bryce asks as I drop my stuff in the sand, then sit in the chair they've pulled up next to Vanessa. "I was just about to go back for another round."

"Oh, I don't know . . ." I say. "Just a lemony sort of soda, I think."

He nods and takes off. Then I lean over to Vanessa and sniff her drink. "What is that?" I whisper.

"Just a wine cooler," she admits. "You won't tell the parental units, will you?"

I shake my head no and look longingly out to the waves. "Has anyone gone surfing yet?" I ask, probably too eagerly.

"Not yet. We usually just sort of hang out and chill for a while. Then it gets livelier, and before long you've got surfing and volley-ball and it's pretty fun."

"You mean after you've all had a few drinks."

"It's not just about drinking, Hannah." She scowls and lowers her voice. "You're not going to act like the goody-goody missionary girl, now are you?"

"No," I tell her. "I'm just curious as to how it all works."

"Here you go, ladies." Bryce hands us both a drink, then sits down again, popping open a fresh beer for himself and taking a long swig.

Vanessa pours the remains of her old drink into the new one, then drops the empty cup in the sand. I take a sip of what I assume is lemon squash with ice, then stop. "What's in this?" I ask Bryce.

"Didn't you say a lemony drink?"

I nod and then sniff my drink. "Is it alcohol?"

He laughs. "Sorry, Hannah. I figured you meant like a lemon drop or something, but the bar selection's kind of limited. That's a club soda with a shot of lemon schnapps in it."

"Is *that* alcohol?" I ask again.

"The schnapps is alcohol. You want me to get you something else?"

I consider this, then take another experimental drink. "No," I tell him. "I'll give this a try."

"Good for you," says Vanessa with obvious relief.

Even so, I don't think it tastes very good, and after a few sips, I give up on it and go off in search of a soda myself. I dig through an Esky until I unearth something called Mellow Yellow and decide to give it a shot. It's not bad, actually, and it doesn't seem to have any alcohol, or if it does it must be minimal. Then I go back to my chair and sit and listen to the others yabbering, mostly about Bryce's recent trip to Europe. But I finish my soda and feel so antsy that I'm sure I can't sit here by the waves for one minute longer. And although there don't seem to be any other surfers out there, I get the feeling we're missing some pretty good wave action.

"I'm going to give it a go," I announce to no one in particular as I get up and pick up my board.

"Good for you," says Bryce.

I turn and look at him. "You a surfer?"

"Nah." He shakes his head. "I'm not really the athletic type."

"He's more the academic type," offers Vanessa with a smile. "Bryce came really close to being valedictorian for his class this year."

I nod. "Good on ya." Then I turn and trudge out to the water's edge. It's not as warm as I expected. But I remind myself that it's not New Guinea either. And in a way, it's refreshing and seems fairly clean, and it doesn't take long to get used to it. I wade out, stopping when it gets about waist deep, and then flop down onto the board and start paddling out. Just relax, I tell myself. Maybe no one is looking.

But I hear squeals of laughter, and I naturally assume they're directed at me as I flop around, falling time and again from my board. After what feels like about an hour and a gallon of ingested sea water, I am ready to give up. But then I see an enticing wave, and for some reason, I think maybe this is *the one*. So I paddle back out, get the board in position, and the next thing I know I am riding! And then I am squatting. And now I am standing, and I'm feeling what has to be about the coolest feeling in the whole wide world. And I look toward the beach and wonder if anyone—please someone!—is watching. But I can't tell, and I know I need to stay focused on my balance and this amazing ride. And so I do. And to my extreme pleasure, I ride it all the way until the wave just fades away and I am in the shallow water again.

"Killer ride!" yells a voice from the beach. I push wet hair from my eyes and look up to see Wyatt approaching me with his own board.

I wave and yell thanks. "It's just getting good," I say when he's closer to me.

"I saw you out here taking a beating," he says as we both push our boards out into the deeper water.

"Yeah," I admit. "I'm pretty rusty. But that last ride gives me hope." Now I get onto my board, somewhat awkwardly, I'm sure. And the next thing I know he is on his, but he does it in one smooth motion, as if this is something he can do in his sleep.

"Hey, it's way cool you're willing to try," he says as we both paddle out. "Most girls wouldn't want to get messed up out here."

I kind of laugh. "Well, I guess I'm not like most girls."

He turns and smiles at me, and I swear I think I'm melting. I mean, that smile is absolutely killer. Those white teeth, all lined up perfectly straight, shining out of his sun-baked face. And those sparkling eyes, the same color as the ocean. Well, I'm not even sure that I'll be able to focus on my surfing anymore today.

We paddle for a while, and I'm relieved that he's not talking. It gives me a chance to gather myself, to just relax and remember the simple steps to a good ride. I really don't want to make an idiot of myself out here in front of him.

"That looks like our ride," he says, suddenly taking off. And now I am paddling furiously, just trying to keep up. But he gets there first and gets into position, and I'm still trying to turn around, trying to get myself to a place where I can start my ride. But it's too late. I am sideways, and I flip over and roll like a sausage while my dream boy zips gracefully past. The story of my life.

But at least my suit stays in place. And when it's all said and done, he seems appropriately sympathetic as well as encouraging. "Sorry about that," he tells me. "I didn't give you much notice. But, man, that was awesome! Did you see the curl on that thing?"

I'm wiping what I hope isn't a big trail of green snot from my nose and trying to regain some sense of dignity as I push wet strands of hair from my eyes. "I guess I wasn't paying attention."

"Well, maybe you should take a break. You've been out here a while."

"Nope. I don't think so. I think I need to get back out there and try harder."

Now we're both paddling out there again, but he's giving me this little pep talk this time. "Maybe that's your problem. Maybe you're trying *too* hard. Maybe you just need to loosen up some. Go with the flow, you know?"

"I know you're right," I admit. "I keep telling myself to just relax. That's how I got that last good ride."

"So do it again," he says. "And remember to breathe."

Then we see another wave rising, and following his lead, I paddle not so furiously this time but with a calm kind of intensity that seems to move me even faster. I can tell I'm keeping up with him. Either that or he is going slow to stay back with me. And then we are there, and he gives me the nod and starts turning around. Reminding myself to loosen up, I follow suit. I remember to breathe, and the next thing I know *I am riding again!* I make it into a squat and then manage to stand upright. And it's even better than the first ride. It's *awesome! Totally awesome!* as Vanessa would say. And I can't wait to do it again.

We ride about a dozen more waves. I take a couple of tumbles and finally realize that I am getting tired.

"You need a rest," Wyatt tells me. "Let's go back in."

And I am so happy that he said "let's" that I offer no resistance as we wade out of the water and drop our boards out of reach of the surf.

"You were great out there," he tells me. "A real surfer girl!"

"Thanks," I say, laughing. "But you're way better. Man, you just make it look so easy."

"That's because it *is* easy."

"Maybe for you." I sigh. "I still have to work at it."

"It's not work," he says. "Remember. It's about loosening up, relaxing, and going with the flow. As soon as you get rigid, you wipe out."

I nod. "Yeah, and remember to breathe."

"Right."

"Thanks for the lesson," I say as I start to head back to Vanessa.

"Do you want to get something to eat?" he asks.

"Oh, yeah," I say. "I guess that sounds good."

So he leads me up to the deck where food of all kinds is spread out, and he hands me a large paper plate. "Go for it," he says.

I start loading my plate. I don't even know what some of these rolled-up things are, but I'm so hungry that I don't really care.

"Way to go," he says when I finally realize that my plate is full and stop. "I like seeing a girl who's not afraid to eat."

I shrug. "Not when I'm feeling this peckish."

"There's an empty table down there," he says, pointing off to the right. And so we go and sit all by ourselves, just pigging out until both our plates are empty.

"I'm going back for more," he says. "How about you?"

I laugh. "No thanks, I'm stuffed. If I eat another bite, I'll sink straight to the bottom of the ocean next go 'round."

"You want anything else to drink? A beer or something?"

Now I consider this. I can see that Wyatt's drinking beer, and it's tempting to try and be like him, but I know that I hate the taste. "I'm not much into beer," I admit.

"A wine cooler then?" he offers. "Lots of girls seem to like those."

"I reckon I can give it a go," I say.

He smiles, then says, "Good on ya!"

I laugh. "Hey, where'd you hear that?"

"I've been around a bit myself," he says in his best Aussie imitation. "Haven't been Down Under just yet, but a few of my surfing mates come from there."

"Well, good on ya!" I toss back at him.

To my surprise, this wine cooler thing's not half-bad. Not as tasty as a lemon squash, but not bad either. Still, I want to be careful and not drink too much. Especially since I plan to surf some more later. I'm not sure, but I think surfing under the influence might be dangerous.

Wyatt and I are in the midst of an interesting conversation about surfing when Felicia suddenly appears. It seems she's been in the house—doing what? Perhaps touching up her already perfect nails? I try not to look at mine. I know Lan's manicure is long gone, and they're chipped and full of sand.

"Wyatt," she says in a tone that suggests ownership. "I've been looking all over for you. I need some help inside."

He nods and stands, then tells me good-bye and vanishes into the beach house with her. To do what? I decide not to let my mind even go there. Who cares what they're doing? Maybe she does just need some help. I clear off our table, toss the remains into the trash, then head back over to where Vanessa and her friends are just starting up a volleyball game.

"You ready to play?" she asks.

"Mind if I scrub up a bit, then take a little rest?" I say. "I just ate a bunch of food, and I'm afraid if I leap around too much I'll chunder for sure."

"That's so cute," says Bree.

Cute? Well, whatever. So I take my bag and head up to the beach house. Is this some kind of excuse? Am I expecting to discover Wyatt and Felicia in there somewhere? Doing something? I'm not sure, and I tell myself that I don't even care. Then a helpful girl shows me to a bathroom where I am able to rinse off some of the sand and crud and pick the seaweed from my hair. Then I change into my dry bikini (which looks a bit more like what the other girls are wearing) and go back outside, where I lay out my Tommy towel and flop down. And despite all the noise and activity around me, I actually fall asleep. I wake up when I feel someone tapping me on the shoulder.

"You ready to play volleyball now?" asks Vanessa. "We need some serious help over here."

So I hop to my feet and walk over to join their team. Vanessa kind of laughs, then points to my cheek. "You've got a towel imprint on your face."

"Great," I tell her. "Thanks for letting me in on that bit of news. Any dried up drool on my chin?" She shakes her head, and then I glance past the net to see that our opponents are none other than Wyatt and Felicia and another couple. I force a sleepy smile to my face, and the games begin.

Now, I've always been fair at sports and fairer than most at volleyball, but I gotta admit these Yanks (well, some of them) are pretty decent. Vanessa is actually holding her own. And despite Bryce's earlier disclaimer about not being athletic, he isn't half-bad either. And the other guy on our team, Andrew Simmons (an African American dude with a crazy sense of humor), is absolutely fantastic. Between him and me, we are keeping our team alive. Because on the other side of the net, it is *all* Wyatt. Oh, sure, Clayton isn't exactly chopped liver, but those two girls—Felicia and Bree—are absolutely useless. No, they are worse than that; they are actually in the way and probably the only reason our team is winning.

Finally the match comes to an end—and our team wins!

"You saved us, Hannah," says Bryce as he slaps my palm.

"Didn't I tell you she was good?" brags my cousin.

"Not only a surfer but a volleyball player too," says Wyatt as he comes around to our side and pats me on the back.

"Speak for yourself," I tell him.

He smiles. "You ready to tackle the waves again?"

"As soon as I get something to drink," I say. And as I walk over to the drink area, I hear Felicia talking to him in this little-girl voice, asking why he wants to go out again.

"Because it's fun," he tells her. "You should try it sometime."

"Yeah, right," she replies in a flat tone.

And for a brief moment, I think that maybe I *am* winning.

thirteen

Wyatt and I and several others surf into the late afternoon. To my relief, I seem to be holding my own out here. And despite my initial delight of being the only girl among all these blokes, I am kind of happy to see a girl coming out to join us. She seems to be the same girl who showed me to the bathroom earlier—one of the few girls who's been genuinely pleasant to me.

"Hey, Jess!" yells Wyatt from where he's straddling his board as we all wait for the next good wave.

"Who's that?" I ask, since I'm only a few feet away from him.

"Jessie," he tells me. "Felicia's younger sister."

I nod, remembering Felicia's comment about how her little sister wore Tommy too. Somehow I'd gotten the impression that her little sister was about eight years old. "How old is she?" I ask Wyatt.

"Just a year younger than Felicia. Their parents call them Irish twins. Jessie's going to be a junior."

"Looks like you guys have been getting some good waves," says Jessie as she paddles up and joins us. Then Wyatt introduces us.

"Oh, yeah," says Jessie. "You're the girl with the cool accent that I met in the house. Nice to meet you, Hannah."

"You too. But I had no idea you were Felicia's sister," I admit.

She chuckles. "Yeah, most people can hardly believe we're

related." Then she makes a face at Wyatt. "Felicia got the looks, and I got the brains."

I frown as I look at her short-cropped, sun-bleached hair, bright eyes, and clear complexion. "Seems to me you *both* got the looks," I say. Of course, I can't say as much for the brains, since I think Felicia is a bit of a nong.

"Hey, I like you already," she says as she paddles up and situates her board right next to mine. "Cool suit, by the way."

I force a smile. "Yeah, your sister told me that you used to like Tommy too." Then I immediately regret my words. I don't want Jessie to think I'm knocking her sister.

But she just laughs. "Yeah, Felice thinks I have absolutely no fashion sense whatsoever. But I think it's all a matter of perspective. I mean, just because she's dumb enough to pay hundreds of dollars for a single item of clothing that she'll wear maybe once and that will be completely out of style by next week . . . well, it doesn't mean I have to do the same. And she's wrong. I didn't *used* to like Tommy. I still like Tommy. And after seeing your suit, I like Tommy even more."

"Here it comes!" yells a voice from behind, and suddenly we're all scrambling to get ready. The next thing I know, we're riding a really huge one. I glance to my left to check on Jessie, and she's just as competent as anyone. She gives me a grin and a thumbs-up, and I'm about to give her one back when *wham!* I get caught in the curl and am flipped head over heels. The surf spins me around a few times, and I finally emerge sputtering and spewing salt water from my mouth and nose.

"That one really cleaned your clock!" yells Jessie from the shallow water where it appears she rode without any trouble.

I shrug and go retrieve my board.

"Going out again?" she calls.

I nod. "Yeah, sure. I can't quit while I'm down."

Fortunately, I manage much better after that. And I enjoy hanging out with Jessie and Wyatt and the other blokes, and I wonder why the rest of the kids at the beach party can't be this much fun.

Finally I notice the sun is getting low in the sky, and a chill runs down my back. I'm not sure if I'm actually cold or having a flashback to the shark book I just read. But I do know for a fact that evening and early morning are the favored hunting times for those beasts. "You guys ever worry about after darks around here?" I call out.

"What's that?" asks Jessie.

"It's Aussie for sharks," says Wyatt.

Jessie squints up at the sky. "It is getting late. We should probably call it a day."

So she and I surf one more wave in, and the blokes (showing off their bravery, I'm sure) give it a couple more goes before they start trickling to shore. Wyatt, of course, is the last one, and he rides in a magnificent wave with the red sky behind him. Our small group of surfers, who are huddled together on the beach like spectators, all clap as he emerges from the water and walks toward us, his board balancing on his shoulder.

"Good on ya, mate!" I tell him as he sticks the end of his board into the dry sand.

He grins. "Good on ya too. You were really looking great out there this afternoon, Hannah."

"Thanks. It's fun getting back into it. I just wish it wasn't so expensive to rent this board, or I'd probably do it every—"

"You *rented* a board?" asks Wyatt.

"That's nuts," adds Jessie. "We've got plenty to share. Don't we, Wyatt?"

"That's for sure." He frowns at me. "Don't waste money renting again."

"In fact, my old Becker would probably be perfect for you," says Jessie.

"Truly?"

She laughs. "Yes, *truly*."

"And there's lots more beaches around here that you should try out," says Wyatt. "You'll have to let us show you around."

"*Who* are you going to show around?" asks Felicia as she joins our damp and slightly bedraggled group. She looks perfect as usual. And she has changed from her bikini to a strapless white sundress. The only thing around her long, tanned neck is a string of green beads that I assume are expensive, but the amazing thing is how perfectly they match her eyes.

"Hannah," says Wyatt as he places a hand on my shoulder. "She's turning into quite the little surfer."

"Yeah," says Jessie. "I can't believe it's been that long since you were on a board. You looked totally great out there."

I kind of shrug and feel self-conscious. "Maybe it's like riding a bike."

"You want to see that board?" offers Jessie.

"Sure," I tell her. "I've heard Beckers are totally bonza."

"Bonza!" she repeats. "I love it!"

I force myself not to look back at Wyatt and Felicia as Jessie and I walk up toward the house. I imagine that he's looking down on her, probably smiling at her absolute perfection. She really is beautiful. But then, looks are only skin-deep.

"Felicia's jealous of you," says Jessie in a confidential tone.

"Of me?" I kind of laugh. "You gotta be kidding."

"No, I'm not. And that means you need to watch out. Felicia can be really possessive of her guys. And right now she thinks Wyatt belongs exclusively to her."

"But I'm not trying to—"

"Oh, it doesn't matter whether you're trying or not, Hannah. Believe me, I think Wyatt would be far better off with someone like you. But Felicia has her claws into him, and I'm sure she won't part with him without a fight."

"A fight?" I turn and look at Jessie, and she just laughs.

"Not an actual kicking and screaming fight. She's way too cool for that. But trust me, Hannah, she will try to get you if she thinks you're in her way."

"You don't sound like you love your sister much."

Jessie sighs. "I do love her. I just don't love what she does. Mostly I'm praying for her—praying that she grows up before it's too late."

"You pray?" I don't know why I find this so shocking. Maybe it's because I assumed there wasn't a single Christian down here in Orange County. But then again, I suppose there are other religions that pray too.

She stops by the Esky chest and grabs a soda. "Want one?"

I nod and go for another Mellow Yellow.

"Yeah, I do pray," she tells me as we go around to a side deck that seems to lead to the garage. "I've been a Christian for three years now. I'm the only one in the family. But I'm praying for everyone to get saved by the time I graduate from high school."

I am not sure whether to admire her or think her a bit whacked. I can't imagine being the only Christian in my family. "Why then?"

She shrugs. "I don't know. I guess so I will feel like I can go away to college or whatever without feeling too worried about them." She pauses to open a door and flick on a light. "The board's in here."

"That's just so weird," I say as I follow her.

"That the board's in here?"

"No." I kind of laugh. "That no one in your family is a Christian, but you are, and you apparently want to be, and that you're praying for them. It's just so weird."

She's pulling a board down from an overhead rack. "This is it," she says. "It's a little beat up. It's the one I learned on, but it's really not bad. You want to borrow it for a while?"

I run my hand over the smooth surface. It's way better than the rental. "I'd love to. Are you sure you're okay with—"

"Yeah. I think ol' Becky's been wishing someone would take her out again."

"Well, I'd be happy to accommodate her."

So we take ol' Becky out to the Jeep and I put her in the back. "Thanks so much, Jessie. I promise to take good care of it."

She nods. "Okay, now back to weird. Why do you think it's so weird that I'm a Christian and my family isn't? Or that I pray for them?"

"It's a rather long story," I admit.

"I've got time," she says as we go back outside and walk around to the back of the house. But for some reason I don't feel like telling her my story just yet. She is reminding me of Sophie. The tiki torches are burning now, and the music is louder than before. People are starting to eat again, and I suspect by the way some of them are walking and talking that they may have had too much to drink. Jessie and I are standing on the deck just watching them. But the night air is starting to get to me, and I'm starting to shiver.

"It's not quite as warm here as what I'm used to," I admit.

"You should get into some dry stuff," she says. "Why don't you go get your bag and come inside and clean up?"

"Sounds great."

This time she shows me to a nicer bathroom upstairs. "There's shampoo and stuff," she tells me. "Use whatever you need."

So I take my time to shower and shampoo the sand and grit from my hair. After seeing Felicia so dressed up, I wish I'd thought to bring something besides beach clothes. All I have are a pair of red Tommy shorts and a striped tank top. But they'll have to do. I fluff my hair up a bit, then put on some lip gloss and mascara. It's not much, but it's more than I would normally do. And really, I don't look so bad, I tell myself as I peer into the slightly fogged-up mirror.

I go downstairs and take my beach bag out to the Jeep where it occurs to me that I've already missed the deadline for returning the rental board, which means I'll have to pay an extra ten bucks if I get it back by nine tomorrow morning. No worries, I tell myself. At least I won't be wasting money on a rental board again. Even so, I go back down to the beach to retrieve it and put it safely away.

"You're not leaving, are you?" calls Wyatt when he spots me from the deck. "The party's just beginning."

I wave at him. "Just putting my board away."

"Come back and have some food," he says. "These salmon wraps are awesome!"

I can see Felicia standing just a few feet from him, and I can tell she is giving me that look. I'd call it narrowed eyes, but she's too clever to let that much expression show on her pretty face. Maybe it's not so much a look as a feeling, but I know that it's real. And I know that Jessie's warning was sincere. But suddenly I'm thinking, *Fine, if Felicia wants to fight, bring it on.*

"Hey," calls Jessie as I come back to the house. "I thought maybe you'd left."

"No chance," I tell her. "Wyatt said there are some awesome salmon wraps out there. Whatever a wrap is."

She explains that they're just little rolled-up sandwiches. "No big deal."

"There's room down here," calls Wyatt, waving to the two of us. "Come on down, surfer girls."

So we go down to the table where Wyatt and Felicia have been sitting by themselves. And I can tell that our company is not welcomed by Felicia. Even so, the rest of us are soon yabbering about the waves and the surf and the last time a shark was spotted in these waters. And then Wyatt starts talking about this girl who got attacked by a shark in Hawaii. "Just snapped off her arm," he says. "Totally took off with it."

"No way," I say, astounded.

"Didn't you hear about it?" asks Jessie. "It was on the news everywhere."

"Not in New Guinea."

"But that's not the end of the story," says Wyatt. "This girl was really into surfing, and as soon as she recovered she went back out."

"That's a brave girl," I say, wondering if I'd be that brave.

"Not only did she go back out," says Jessie, "but she won some surfing championship, like about three months later."

"Amazing!" I say.

"Yes, isn't it?" says Felicia, but I can tell she's being sarcastic.

Jessie gives me a glance that I suspect means "I told you so." But I just smile. "Do you ever surf, Felicia?"

"Oh, I used to, back when I was little and there wasn't much else to do. It was a way to beat the boredom."

I nod. "How do you beat the boredom now?"

She looks at me and blinks. "What?"

"What keeps you from being bored now?"

She kind of laughs, like she's indulging a dimwit. "Oh, there's lots to do now. I mean, I have my own car and I can go wherever I want and—"

"Where do you like to go?"

"Oh, lots of places. There's Laguna—"

"What do you do in Laguna?" I say quickly. "Isn't that a surfing area?"

"Well, yes, but it's more than just a beach. There's lots to do."

"Like what?" I ask innocently.

"Well, the shops for instance. There are lots of great shops down there."

I nod. "So you spend a lot of time shopping?"

"Well, not a lot of time . . ."

"Ha!" says Jessie. "Shopping is Felicia's favorite pastime."

"That's right," chimes in Wyatt. "And the stores just love to see her coming too. They actually know her by name."

"Oh, Wyatt," she says, all charm. "That's not really true." Then she waves over to where some new people are coming out onto the deck. "Hey, Shelby and Blake!" she calls. "Come on over here. I want you to meet my boyfriend." And suddenly she's standing, and a very sophisticated-looking couple is being introduced, and it's as if Jessie and I have been excused.

"The children's hour is over," whispers Jessie as we go find another place to sit.

"That's fine by me. I think I've had enough for one night."

"So you see what I mean then? About the way Felicia fights?"

"Was that round one?"

"I think so. And even though you were doing pretty well, I don't think you won. I don't even think it's over."

I shrug and pick up another salmon wrap. "It's over for me."

Jessie just laughs. "You want to come back here tomorrow to surf again?"

"Really?" I ask.

"Yeah. I thought I'd come after church and hang out here. It's fairly quiet on Sundays since my dad usually takes the boat out."

"That's right," I say. "I heard you guys have this awesome sailboat. Why don't you go out with him?"

"He leaves too early. I'd miss church."

Now this really throws me for a loop. "You give up sailing to go to church?" I ask.

"Of course." Then she smiles. "But it's not like I don't believe you can have fun on Sundays. And I sure wouldn't mind catching a few more waves."

So it's arranged. We'll meet here around noon. Even so, I can't quite figure this girl out. And as I look around this party that's being hosted at her parents' house and notice the easy flow of alcohol, I can't help but wonder how this makes her feel.

"It seems funny that you'd want to come to this party," I finally say.

"Why's that?"

"Well, with you being a Christian and everyone drinking and all. It doesn't make sense."

"Yeah, I used to feel like that. But then I realized that first, not everyone is drinking, and second, maybe Jesus can use me being here. Like I'll have a conversation with someone, and they'll end up coming to church with me and getting saved." She smiles. "That's pretty cool. And besides that, I guess I feel kind of responsible since this is my family's property, and I'm personally quite fond of this house. I don't want to see things getting out of hand." She leans in as if to tell a secret. "I had to call the police once to get them to empty the place out when a couple of guys started acting like complete morons."

"So you're a bit like security?"

She laughs. "I guess you could say that."

I glance around the decks and beach, curious as to whether anything is going to get out of hand tonight, but the crowd, though boisterous, seems rather calm. And some couples, including Wyatt and Felicia, are actually starting to dance. I try not to look like I'm staring, but I can't help but watch as the two of them cling to each other. It all looks very romantic, and I have a feeling that Jessie is right. Felicia has won round one.

So I tell Jessie good night, then find Vanessa and Bryce, kissing as it turns out, and with some embarrassment I tell them that I'm going home.

"But the night is still young," says Bryce as he adjusts his glasses, which I reckon are all steamed up.

"Maybe for some," I say as I wave and walk away. But not for me.

fourteen

"You are not going to believe this," says Jessie as soon as I show up at the beach house. She's just parked her car, a sporty little red thing, in the driveway, and she's dressed nicely, as if she's just come from church.

"What?" I ask as I unload my (rather, her) board.

"Wyatt and Felicia got into a really big fight."

"For real?" I lean the board against the Jeep and wait. "When?"

"Last night. After you left. And do you know what they were fighting about?"

I shrug.

"You!"

Now, this makes me laugh. "Me? Seriously?"

She nods. "Go ahead and take the board around back, and I'll unlock the house. I'm sure it's still a big mess."

As I take the board around back, I can see that it is indeed a big mess. An even bigger mess than when I left. I drop the board in the sand, then head up the deck, gathering paper plates and cups as I go and tossing them into one of the large rubbish bins that had obviously gone unobserved.

"Don't worry about that," she says as she opens the back door to let me in. "That's Felicia's responsibility."

"Does she clean it up?"

Jessie laughs. "Yeah, you bet. No, she has some people come in. Later today, I think."

"Where is she now?" I ask, glancing nervously around the house just in case she's lurking somewhere, ready to pounce on me and knock me flat.

"She's sailing with *Daddy*."

I nod and wonder why the emphasis on *daddy*. Jessie is rummaging through the fridge and finally pulls out a plate of cold cuts and cheese, I'm guessing salvaged from last night. She then finds a box of crackers and sets these on the bar between us. "Want a soda?"

"Sure."

"As I mentioned before, it's their Sunday thing . . . sailing." She wrestles a couple cans of soda from a box, then sets them on the bar. "Sprite okay?"

"Great."

"Felicia, as you may have guessed, is *Daddy's* favorite. In his eyes, she can do no wrong. I, on the other hand, am a complete disappointment."

"How's that?"

"Mostly because of religion. He sees my Christian beliefs as a direct challenge to his own ways of thinking and living. Plus he always assumes that I don't respect him."

"Do you?"

She seems to consider this. "I respect him as my father. But I guess I don't really respect his views or values. I honestly think money is his god. Well, that and beautiful women. He's on his fourth wife now."

"Where's your mother?"

"She died about ten years ago. And in Daddy's defense, he did

stay with her until she died. But he was married within the year."
She puts a piece of cheese on a cracker. "A wannabe actress named
Holly. Then there was Krista. She had been a 'lingerie model,' which
I think was just another word for stripper. Now he's married to
number four, Carrie. She's actually the best one of the bunch in some
ways. But I know for a fact she wouldn't have married my dad if he
hadn't been rich. And of course, he never would've married her if
she hadn't been beautiful. That's how it works in my family. Beauty
and money—the perfect combination. But neither of those interests
me much."

"Wow."

"But I'm getting sidetracked," she says suddenly. "I was telling
you about Felicia and Wyatt's big fight. I can't believe Vanessa didn't
fill you in."

"I'd already gone to bed when she got home, and then I left
before she was up. I had to return the rental surfboard before nine.
Then I just drove around, did some sightseeing, you know."

"Right. Well, Felicia was trying to talk Wyatt into going sailing
with her again today, but he said he wanted to go surfing instead.
And that just really ticked her off. She goes, 'You'd rather surf on
your stupid board than go sailing with me?' And then it just got
worse. Before long, she was accusing him of having some kind of
fling with you—like you and he were out there getting it on while
you were surfing. Yeah, right! But he defended you, saying you were
a nice girl with missionary parents—" Now Jessie stops and studies me with her can of soda suspended in midair. "Your parents are
really missionaries?"

I nod with, I'm sure, a guilty expression.

"Wow, I never would've guessed that. Anyway, Felicia just got
madder and madder and finally Wyatt just stomped out. But then

Felicia started acting like everything was just fine. She went around telling everyone that she was done with Wyatt, saying things like, 'He was just a parasite anyway' and 'All he's interested in is money.' You know, stupid stuff like that."

"So you think they're really finished?"

Jessie shrugs. "I wouldn't bet on it. I think Felicia really likes Wyatt a lot. I actually heard her crying in her room last night. I asked if she wanted to talk, but she just told me to leave her alone."

"I feel kind of bad."

"Don't," says Jessie quickly. "Trust me, Felicia's not done with this thing yet. And besides, wait until you hear the rest."

"There's more?"

She nods with a somber expression. "A lot of the kids kept on drinking. Including your cousin and Bryce. In fact, I think Vanessa got a little sick to her stomach because she went in the house and was in the bathroom for quite a while. And guess what?"

"What?"

"While Vanessa was in there, puking or whatever, Felicia enticed Bryce to dance with her. And I'm not sure if Bryce really knew what he was doing, but by the time Vanessa came back out, Felicia and Bryce were dancing like they were glued to each other."

"Oh, no."

"Oh, yes. So Vanessa and Bryce had a little fight. Actually, he kept apologizing, and she was crying. And then they went home."

Poor Vanessa. That couldn't have been much fun for her. And in a way it was my fault. Or was it?

"So you missed the fireworks," says Jessie as she gathers up what's left of our snack and shoves it into the fridge. "Ready to surf now?"

"Sure," I say.

"Let me get ready, and I'll meet you down there."

So while I'm waiting for Jessie, despite her telling me not to bother with it, I find myself automatically cleaning up. I don't even know why. But I actually feel better seeing that the deck doesn't look like a dump site.

"You didn't have to do that," she says as she catches me tossing the last pile of rubbish into the bin. "But thanks."

Then we go out and surf until we're tired and cold. But I can tell that I'm improving, and I know the Becker board is part of it. "That was so great," I tell Jessie as the two of us flop down in the hot, dry sand and soak up some afternoon sun.

"That was totally awesome."

"You are so lucky to have a place like this," I say, trying not to sound too envious.

"I guess so," she says. "But it's kind of a mixed blessing, you know?"

I sigh. "I think I kind of know."

"Okay, I've told you a lot about my parents. Now I want to hear about yours."

So I decide it's no big deal and tell her the story. How my parents met at translation school. How they both wanted to go to a Third World country. How they got married and spent the latter part of their honeymoon in what is known as "jungle camp" and how my brothers and I were born later. "It's almost like we were an intrusion," I say to her as I stare up at the cloudless sky overhead. I realize I've never said this before and feel guilty saying it now.

"How's that?"

"Well, I love my parents, and I know they love me, but they were always so focused on the language and the village and all the various ways that they wanted to improve life for the people—starting schools, getting medical help, and whatnot—that I sometimes reckon we kids just got in the way."

Jessie sits up now. "Seriously?"

"Sort of. Oh, I'll admit it was fun growing up in the village. And I loved it when we were all there together, but it seems like that ended so quickly. I was only seven when my oldest brother went off to attend school on the mission base, and two years later I was the only kid at home. Then I was sent off to school when I was twelve, and it was great being with my brothers again for a bit, but by the end of that year Matthew was off to uni—college, I mean." I sigh and sit and look at Jessie. "Our family still got together for holidays and furlough and breaks. But sometimes I think we missed out on so much. Like I see Vanessa and her parents and how they all live together. Well, sort of. They do tend to go off on their own a lot—sort of doing their own thing in their great big house."

"That's pretty much how my family is too. I'm sure outsiders see us and think we're all happy and close—because my dad tries to create that image. But in reality we're all like ships passing in the night." She sifts sand through her fingers and lets it pour over her feet. "I think you might just be doing that old 'grass is greener' thing, Hannah. I felt jealous when I first heard your parents were missionaries. I mean, I wondered, *Why couldn't that be my parents?*"

Now, this is news. I laugh. "And I'm sure I've been thinking the same thing about Vanessa's parents. And probably yours too, although I haven't met them. But hearing stories of your dad's sailing trips on Sundays, and then this beach house. Well, it just looks so great."

"Looks can be deceiving."

"Right."

"So if your parents are missionaries, Hannah . . . uh, do you mind if I ask, well . . ."

"You mean what happened to me?"

She nods.

"You're wondering if having missionary parents means that I'm a Christian too?"

"It crossed my mind."

I lean forward, putting my elbows on my knees and feeling the gritty grains of sand embedding into my skin. "I'm not really sure anymore."

"Anymore? Meaning you used to be?"

"Right." So then I give her my brief spiritual history, telling how I'm sort of taking a holiday from God and how I didn't bring my Bible to the States and how my best mate Sophie is all worried that I'm going to hell in Orange County.

"And maybe it's true," I say. "For instance, I wondered about some of those tumbles I took in the surf yesterday—some felt pretty gruesome—and I wondered what if I'd been sucked down and unable to come up?"

"Like where would you be right now?"

"Yeah, that thought actually went through my head."

"So where do you think you'd be?" she asks in a quiet voice.

I shrug. "Well, I still believe in God. And I did give my heart to Jesus, it seems like about a hundred years ago. So I reckon I'd be in heaven."

"Well, I think you'd be in heaven too."

I sigh, feeling slightly relieved.

Then she looks closely at me. "But you're not so sure?"

"Not entirely. I mean, I know all about the daily things, like praying and reading your Bible and going to church and that stuff. I've been doing it all my life."

"I think God has even more for us."

"More? What if I don't want more?"

Jessie seems to weigh this. Finally she says, "Maybe that's just because you don't know the kind of *more* I'm talking about. But I think there's a reason for that too."

"What?"

"I think it's because you've been pushing God away, and if you continue to ignore him and don't read his Word or spend any time with other Christians—well, I think it'll just make it way easier for you to turn your back on him for good."

I nod, and as much as I hate to admit it, I think she's right. "Yeah, I kind of think the same thing. When I think about it, that is, which hasn't been a lot in these past several weeks."

"Sounds like you've been doing some thinking to me."

"Not consciously, though. I reckon most of my thinking has been kind of subconscious or maybe at some other level."

"Like a spiritual level?"

"Yeah, maybe."

"Well, I think you're going to be just fine, Hannah."

And for some reason, I find that a bit reassuring. Not that I reckon Jessie's any kind of expert in these matters. The fact is, I've probably had way more Christian teaching than she has. And yet she has this level of confidence that I don't think I've ever had. More astonishing than that is the way she's made her choice to serve God despite her family's hostility. Wow, I can't imagine what Sophie would think if I told her all the things I've been doing and seeing and thinking lately. I'm sure she'd be praying overtime for me.

Jessie and I get warmed up enough to surf a bit more, and I'm starting to think that surfing is a great way to block all these troubling thoughts from my mind. It's like I can just empty myself out when I'm riding a wave, like I become a part of the ocean or a piece of driftwood or a seabird or something. No worries.

Finally we're both too tired to keep going, and I suspect I should get home anyway. For one thing, I'm feeling guilty about Vanessa, as if I'm somehow responsible for how things went with her and Bryce last night. And besides that, I need to be ready for work in the morning.

"Thanks for everything," I tell Jessie. "It's been truly amazing."

"You're welcome to come out and surf whenever you like," she says. "In fact, you can just leave the board here if you want."

"Do you surf every day?"

She shakes her head. "No. I'd like to surf more, but my dad made me promise not to surf alone."

"I reckon I can help you in that regard. I even took a class on lifesaving when I was fourteen."

She laughs. "That's reassuring. But seriously, surfing has been so awesome for me these past two days. Sometimes it almost feels like a form of worship."

"Surfing as a form of worship?" I study this strange girl and feel the need to scratch my head.

"Yeah. Like it's me and God, just hanging together. Pretty cool. If it wasn't for my dad getting all freaked, I'd be tempted to surf by myself. So seriously, anytime you want to come out, just give me a call."

"I work until two during the week."

"Hey, that's pretty much my schedule too. Except I only work till one."

"You work?"

"Not exactly. I volunteer. There's this children's home that our church runs. It's for kids with HIV. During the summer I'm helping out there every day. It's been pretty cool."

"Wow, that's really nice of you."

"Hey, trust me, I get back way more than I give. The kids are awesome."

I nod. "Well, it's still really nice."

So we exchange cell phone numbers and plan to meet here tomorrow afternoon.

"And I can take you to some other good spots too," she says as I'm leaving. "I mean, our beach is okay, but when you get better you might be ready for some bigger challenges."

And I reckon I am ready for some bigger challenges. But not just in surfing. Suddenly I have this hopeful feeling about Wyatt. I can't believe he and Felicia broke up last night—and over me!

fifteen

"WHERE'VE YOU BEEN?" DEMANDS VANESSA WHEN I COME INTO THE house.

"Surfing," I say as I set down my beach bag. "I left a note."

"Yeah, but that was hours ago."

"Well, I figured you'd probably get up around noon or later . . . and then I figured that you and Bryce would be doing something." Maybe I should let her tell me as much as she wants to and play dumb about the rest. I go to the fridge for a soda.

"Bryce is taking his grandma to an afternoon concert," she says in a huffy voice. "As if I care."

"Where are your parents?"

"I don't know. A movie or something."

"Oh."

"Who were you surfing with anyway? Wyatt?"

"Jessie VanHorn."

"Felicia's *little* sister."

"Jessie's sixteen. Just a year younger than we are."

"Yeah, maybe, but she's kind of immature."

I shrug. "I think she's just fine and a good surfing mate."

"And she's religious," says Vanessa, as if that's another point against her. "Maybe she's more like the friends you're used to."

151

I lean my elbows on the countertop and just look at her. "Why are you so sniggly today?"

She kind of laughs. "Sniggly. I like that. And it's exactly how I feel."

I nod. "Jessie filled me in a bit . . . about how Felicia moved in on Bryce last night . . . after you got tanked."

"Tanked?"

"You know, hammered, drunk, plastered, smashed."

Now she actually does laugh. "*Hammered? Tanked?* You crack me up, Hannah. See, this is why I needed you to come home. I was so depressed and lonely, and just hearing your cute little Aussie accent and seeing your rosy cheeks . . . man, Hannah, it looks like you're gonna have a nasty sunburn. Don't you use any sunblock when you're surfing?"

I shrug.

"That's gonna kill your complexion. Not to mention give you skin cancer. You should take better care of yourself."

"I'll be alright."

"Well, it's almost four o'clock. What are we going to do to cheer me up?"

"What do you want to do?"

She gets an impish smile now. "Shopping?"

I start to protest, but she stops me.

"Hey, it's partly your fault that I'm feeling — what was it? Sniggly!"

"Why's that?"

"Wyatt and Felicia got in a fight because Felicia thinks he's got the hots for you."

"The hots?"

She presses her lips together and nods "Yeah, Felicia was just sure you two were doing more than surfing out there yesterday."

"Felicia is such a dill."

Her eyebrows go up. "Maybe so. But I'm not so sure that Wyatt doesn't like you, Hannah. And I'm so mad at Felicia for her little dirty-dancing act with Bryce that I actually hope that Wyatt does like you. It would serve her right."

"But I thought you said that Felicia always gets what Felicia wants."

"Maybe it's time things changed." She points her finger at me now. "And you owe me one, cousin, so go change into something respectable because we're going shopping! And hurry, the good stores will close by six."

So I'm not surprised that Vanessa takes us straight to her favorite shopping center. And while her usual style of shopping feels more like an endurance test for a marathon, today we have more of a sprint. Or maybe it's vengeance shopping. I'm beginning to think I should start categorizing the various shopping styles I've observed during the past few weeks. This afternoon, Vanessa walks quickly, talks quickly, and seems obsessed with finding something that will take away the sting of last night's humiliation.

"Oh, sure he apologized to me," she says as we walk past a fountain to reach the other side of the mall. "And he said that it was all Felicia's doing, which I don't doubt. But it still hurt, Hannah. And I am leaving my cell phone off all day—just in case he tries to call and apologize again. I want him to worry a little."

"Right."

We go into a Via Spiga shop (a name I recognize because of my raincoat, although this store has only shoes and accessories), and she starts looking at shoes, then finally says, "I'm not in a shoe mood" and quickly turns around and leaves. I am trailing her like a hound dog.

Now she goes into one of her favorite clothing boutiques (that one with the French name I can't even pronounce). She moves more slowly now but with just as much obsession. Finally she finds a few things she wants to try on.

"You take something in too, Hannah," she insists.

Remembering that I am partially to blame for her sniggly mood, I don't protest when she picks out several things for me to try. Besides, it doesn't cost anything to try clothes on. And today I'm wearing real designer clothes and don't feel quite so much as if I'm under the microscope as before. In fact, the salesclerk is rather civilized toward me, if not actually polite.

"Let's see," calls Vanessa after a few minutes.

I'm rather surprised that I actually like a couple of things she's picked out for me. I've got on a low-cut skirt that fits just right. At first I thought the print was too bold, but the fabric feels fantastic, and the way it sways so gracefully makes me feel like dancing. Plus, the cut makes me look both taller and slimmer. Quite stylish really. And the top, which is about the same color as a mango, is perfect too. I open the dressing-room door and go out to show her, holding my arms out and strutting like a runway model, feeling the skirt swishing across my legs.

"Oh, Hannah!" she exclaims. "You look so hot in that outfit."

I can't help but grin. "I know. It's rather nice, isn't it?"

"Nice? It's awesome. You are getting it!"

Of course, I never looked at the price tags. Why bother, since I know it's far too much for my pocketbook anyway? "No, I can't possibly get it," I tell her.

"Yes, you can," she insists. "You're a working girl now and I know you got a draw yesterday."

"How much are they?" I ask as I try to find the tags, which seem to have vanished. I think Vanessa said they were Iceberg, which is another word for outrageously expensive.

"Never mind that. You *have* to get this outfit. I almost forgot to tell you. There's another party next Friday, a surprise birthday party for Clayton Stewart—"

"The volleyball guy?"

She laughs. "Right, the volleyball guy. Anyway, Bryce and I are planning it, and you've *got* to come, and you've *got* to wear that outfit."

The salesclerk steps in now. "How is everything?"

"She is absolutely getting that outfit," says Vanessa.

The clerk nods. "It looks fantastic on you. And that color with your hair and your tan is spectacular—"

"She needs to stay out of the sun, though," says Vanessa in a hushed voice, as if I'm not even here. "It's going to ruin her complexion."

The clerk nods. "Yes. We've got a new skin-care line you should look into," she tells me. "Might help even that out."

"But seriously," says Vanessa, "you look totally awesome in that outfit. If we find the right sandals and accessories, you're going to make Wyatt forget about Felicia forever. I promise you."

I frown now. "You think Wyatt really cares about how girls dress?"

She looks at me like I've gone daft. "Of course. How else do you think Felicia got his attention? Her wonderful personality?" I have to laugh at that.

"Wyatt's got good taste, Hannah. And even though his family is having some financial difficulties at the moment, that boy is used to the best, and eventually things will even out for them. But if you want to compete with someone like Felicia VanHorn, you've got to look the part. And you've got to get that outfit." She looks down at what she's tried on and frowns. "And this is definitely not going to work."

I nod and go back into the dressing room and look at my reflection again. I can't deny that this outfit is awesome. But when I remove the garments, carefully, I find the tags. While I'm not shocked, since I've been down this road with Vanessa and Aunt Lori before, I know that they are too much for me. Feeling disappointed, I put them, carefully again, back on the hangers and go back out.

"What do you think of this top?" asks Vanessa hopefully.

"It's nice," I tell her.

"Just nice?"

"No, it's actually rather lovely. And the stripes are quite slimming."

She smiles now. "That's what I thought too. I guess I'll get it."

I'm just putting my things back on the rack when the salesclerk appears. "I thought you wanted to get those," she says.

"Oh, I do," I tell her. "I just can't afford them."

She smiles. "Oh, it shouldn't be about the money. Didn't you see how awesome you looked in that outfit? You're young and pretty, and you should enjoy that great shape while you've got it."

I glance at her, and while she's older, maybe even thirty, she doesn't look too bad herself. "Do you ever have sales?" I ask meekly.

"This Iceberg line just came in. It's actually for fall. I can't imagine it would go on sale for quite some time." She laughs. "And by then it would be gone."

Now Vanessa appears. "I want this top, and she's getting that outfit."

"But Vanessa—"

"No *buts*, Hannah. It looked stunning on you. You've got to have it."

I finger the supple fabric for a moment, wondering how they make fabric so soft and pretty. Then I imagine Wyatt looking at me in this outfit—in that same way I've seen him look at Felicia before. And then I imagine Felicia seeing him looking at me like that. And, well, that just cinches the deal. "Okay," I say, "I'll get them."

Before we leave the shop, I'm enticed to purchase not only the two items but also a necklace and bracelet that both Vanessa and the clerk agree is perfect for the outfit and some skin-care products as well. The grand whopping total is $786.88. My hands shake as I write out the check. The clerk has to help me in filling out the blank counter check.

"Don't worry," says Vanessa. "It's good. My dad just gave her a draw yesterday."

Even so, the clerk has me show her my identification and put Vanessa's charge card number on the back of my check. "Just in case there's a problem," she assures us.

I think I'm in shock when we go looking for shoes—it's back to Via Spiga again—but I don't argue. And to be honest, although I'm in shock, I feel pretty good too. I can't quite describe the feeling exactly, but it's kind of like having power. Realizing that I can go and buy an outfit like this, one that's every bit as nice as the kinds of things Felicia wears, makes me feel like we're on the same playing field or something. And I think I'm feeling somewhat elated. Kind of a high, which makes me wonder if shopping is similar to taking drugs. Is it possible to become addicted?

"Those shoes are perfect," proclaims Vanessa when I try on a strappy pair with fairly high heels. "They make your legs look like they go on forever." Then she frowns. "But we've got to get you in for a pedicure. No way can you wear shoes like that with toenails like those."

I curl my toes to try to cover up the chipped-up polish. "Must've been all the surfing."

"Right."

"She'll take those," she tells the shoe salesman.

And so I write another check, this one for just over $200. My hands aren't shaking so badly now, but I still feel this sense of nervous energy. Almost as if I'm committing a crime. Although I know that I'm not. I mean, I deposited the money yesterday. Still, I can't help but realize that the $2,000 draw from yesterday is down to less than half that now. I take in a deep breath and smile as I thank the salesman and leave.

"Isn't this fun?" says Vanessa as we go to another one of her favorite stores.

I smile and nod. "Yeah," I say, "it actually is."

By the end of our shopping trip, Vanessa has found several items that seem to have pacified her anger, and she's talked me into getting a new purse. "That orange thing from Ross is just not cutting it," she told me. And I had to agree. So I wrote another check for $259 to buy a real Prada purse (it had been marked down from $429). "It's a steal," Vanessa assured me. "It's only on sale because it was part of the spring line. But trust me, it's a very cool style."

Then we stop to get a bite to eat. Vanessa treats, which is something of a relief because I'm starting to feel a bit worried about how quickly my money is disappearing. I've only worked one week, and what I've earned so far won't even cover my draw. Still, I decide not to think about that. Instead I will think about Wyatt and how I plan to win his heart.

sixteen

I HAVE TO ADMIT THAT GOING TO WORK WITH MY NEW PRADA PURSE IN tow did make me feel like a million bucks this week. Both Carlita and Laticia noticed it right away on Monday. Then during break time I told them about the new outfit I bought on Sunday, giving them all the great details, and they were very enthused.

"Way to go, girlfriend," said Laticia as she gave me a high five. "You're going to be one hot mama come Friday night."

"Have someone take a photo," encouraged Carlita. "Then bring it back to show us."

"Better yet," added Laticia with a wink, "why don't you just bring us along?"

Cynthia was off to the side, frowning. "You aren't getting in over your head, are you, Hannah?"

The break room got quiet as I considered this. "No." I said as confidently as possible. "I had the cash to cover it. I didn't even use my cards. And I'm not planning on buying anything else," I said with what I hoped sounded like true conviction.

"That's what you told me last week."

I sort of shrugged. "Well, I'm done now." But on Tuesday Jessie and I stopped at a surf shop, and I bought a new bikini. At least it was on sale, and Mac, the guy who runs the place, guaranteed that it would stay put, even during the worst sort of wipeout.

"And if it doesn't?" asked Jessie, who was skeptical.

"Then kudos to the lucky dudes who are around to witness it!" he said.

So far the suit has stayed on. I met up with Wyatt and Jessie yesterday at Jessie's beach house, and I had on the new bikini, which I think caught Wyatt's eye. In any case, I felt like I had his undivided attention.

Although we only surfed for a little while, we had a great time, and it was fantastic to see him. Even so, we all agreed that the wave action wasn't too impressive.

"You gotta let me take you to Sleepy Hollow," he told me suddenly. Then I guess he remembered Jessie was there too. "It's great, isn't it, Jess? We should all go over there together and catch some waves."

"Sounds great," I told him. "When?"

He looked at his watch and frowned. "Not today. It's getting too late. But how about tomorrow?" Then he told us where to meet him (near the same place where I got my surfing bikini), and it was settled.

I suppose that's another reason I dressed up a bit more than usual for work today. And as I'm driving the Jeep with the top down, wearing my Fendi shirt and my Armani pants, my beach bag full of goodies and my Becker board in back—I am once again feeling like a million bucks. And I'm feeling more and more like I belong here. Other than my accent, which is fading, I think I can pass for a California girl. Oh, I'm not as cool as Vanessa or Felicia, but I can hold my own with Jessie. Not that she makes me work too hard at that. In fact, of all the people I know here, she seems the most genuine. But maybe she doesn't have to try so hard since she's rich. I'm not sure.

When I pull into the parking lot where we planned to meet, I feel like I'm starring in my own movie as I climb from the Jeep, push the hair from my face, adjust my shades, and wave toward where Wyatt and Jessie are waiting.

"We're having smoothies," calls Jessie from where she's standing in line at a kiosk. "What do you want?"

Wyatt comes up to greet me, surprising me with a big hug. "You look mahvahlous, dahling," he says with an appreciative grin. "But I thought we were going surfing."

"I just got off work," I tell him. "Haven't had a chance to change yet."

"I bet Mac will let you change in there," he says, pointing to Mac's Shack.

"Yeah, I'm sure he will since he's the one who talked me into buying this guaranteed-never-to-wipe-out bikini."

"And was he right?" I can see a glimmer of mischievous hope in his eyes.

"So far."

"Too bad."

I playfully sock him in the arm and go over to talk to Jessie.

"What're you having?" I ask her.

"I'm having the ginger orange and Wyatt's having the key lime."

I consider this. "I'll have the key lime too," I tell her as I dig a five out of my wallet. "I'm going into Mac's Shack to change."

She laughs. "Make sure that curtain's closed. You know how Mac is."

So I run back to the Jeep, grab my bag, and go into Mac's Shack.

"Oh, no!" he says when he sees me. "Don't tell me it came off."

"No. I'm perfectly happy with it."

"Whew." He acts dramatically relieved. "So maybe I can sell you another?"

"Actually, I was hoping I could use a dressing room. I'm straight off work and we're going surfing and—"

"Help yourself." He waves me to the back. *"Mi casa es su casa."*

I can hear him whistling as I change, which is something of a relief since it tells me he's up front in the shop, and I'm still not sure whether Jessie's joke was factual or not. I take care with my nice shirt and pants, carrying them over my arm like a fancy waiter would as I go back outside.

"Now that's better," he says when he sees me emerge. I've got a pair of low-rise Tommy shorts over my bikini but still feel a bit exposed, although most girls don't even bother with shorts. I think I'm still a bit old-fashioned.

"Hey, Mac," calls Wyatt as he comes into the shadowy shop. "What's up?"

"I got those new Billabong shades you were asking for."

"No way."

"Way."

"Man, I gotta see those."

So, wondering what Billabong shades are, I follow Wyatt and Mac over to the sunglasses racks. Mac pulls out a pair and holds them up.

"Man, those are even better than I thought." Wyatt tries them on and turns to show me. "Pretty cool, huh?"

"Very cool," I say as I pick up a similar pair. "And I actually like the name a bit too."

"I reckon you would, mate."

Then I slip the sunglasses on and show him.

"Alright," he says as he gives me a thumbs-up. "Way better than those old blue things you've been wearing."

I don't let it show that his insult hurts me. Maybe, like Felicia, he's not a Tommy fan. Then I take off the Billabongs and look for the price. "How much are they, Mac?"

"Let me go look. I just got 'em in and haven't even put the price on yet." So we follow him back to a cluttered counter where he digs out some papers, puts on some glasses, and tries to figure it out. "Looks like they'll run you sixty bucks."

"Each?" I say stupidly.

Mac laughs. "That's not a bad price considering I've got some Oakleys under the counter that go for more than $200."

"Yeah, I've got a pair of those," says Wyatt. "But they're too nice for surfing. These Billabongs are perfect."

I try them on again and go over to the window to look outside. "They do fit nicely," I say, giving my head a shake. "I like how they wrap around and don't let any sun in."

"Tell you what," says Mac. "I'll give you a discount if you both buy a pair. Say 10 percent off? How's that sound?"

"I'm a little short on cash today, Mac," says Wyatt in a wistful voice. "But thanks for the offer."

"Oh, right," I say as I walk up to the counter. "I lose my discount just because Wyatt's not getting his today?" I set my clothes aside and pull out my checkbook. Then I turn to Wyatt. "Why don't you let me get them for you?"

"Oh, I couldn't—"

"Look, you can pay me back later if you'd like. But that way we both get the discount and you can have your sunnies today."

He smiles and turns to Mac. "Isn't my little Aussie girl the greatest?"

So I pay Mac, and Jessie arrives with the drinks in a tray just as we're leaving. "That took like forever," she says. "Hey, nice shades."

"You want some?" asks Wyatt. "Mac will probably give you the group discount."

"Nah," she says. "I've got some that work just fine."

"Can I lock my stuff in your car?" I ask Jessie. "I forgot that I've got the top down and—"

"Why don't you put them in my car?" says Wyatt. "Then we can put all the boards on top of the Jeep and ride together. I've got lots of bungee cords in back."

So I put my things in the backseat of his sporty blue Honda, trying not to snoop as I do it. But all I see are a wadded-up beach towel, which probably can't smell too great, a pair of rubber thongs, and a beat-up ball cap. Nothing too revealing. And the next thing I know I am driving the Jeep with Wyatt next to me and Jessie in the backseat. We're all drinking our smoothies, and I feel alive and carefree and excited.

"You like key lime too?" asks Wyatt.

I nod. "Yeah, it's really bonza."

He holds up his cup. "To bonza!"

Sleepy Hollow turns out to be really great and not too crowded either. "It's way better to come during the week," says Wyatt as we paddle out. Then he turns and grins at me. "Cool shades, Hannah."

I laugh as I admire his matching ones. "Cool shades, Wyatt."

"Thought you called them sunnies."

"Right-o. Cool sunnies! Ya feel better now?"

He nods. "Hey, Jess, don't you feel left out of the club without Billabong shades?"

She kind of laughs. "I'm not sure I want to be in that particular club."

Now I'm feeling a bit guilty, like maybe I'm making her feel left out. So for the rest of the afternoon, I sort of bob back and forth between them, hoping that I'm keeping them both happy. Finally we've done about all the damage possible to that lovely beach and decide it's time to get going.

We're all rather quiet as I drive us back to the meeting spot, so I turn on the radio. "I'm not sure what the best station is," I say to Wyatt. "What do you listen to?"

So he changes it and turns it up, and although it's not my favorite sort of music (a bit too much head thumping going on), I pretend to like it.

"I've got to run," says Jessie as soon as we're back. "I completely forgot that I'm supposed to have dinner with the folks tonight, and Carrie gets grumpy if people are late. Not that I blame her; she's a pretty good cook. This was great! Let's do it again."

"Definitely," says Wyatt as he removes her board and gives it to her.

"See you tomorrow?" I call as she takes off.

"Yeah, later, Hannah."

"What's tomorrow?" asks Wyatt as he takes down his own board and leans it against the Jeep.

"Oh, you know, there's that party for Clayton's eighteenth birthday."

"Yeah, I almost forgot. Bryce called me about that this week. And you're going?"

"According to my cousin I am."

He comes around to where I'm still sitting in the driver's seat. "So you and she and Bryce are doing a little threesome or something?"

I make a face at him. "Hardly."

"Why don't I take you then?" He's leaning against the driver's-side door now, his face only inches from mine.

I try to make an expression that suggests the thought hadn't already occurred to me. "That'd be awesome."

"Or bonza?"

I laugh. "Yeah, that would be totally bonza."

"Bonza," he says again. "I'm really liking that word."

"Well, I better go," I say, suddenly uncomfortable. "Thanks for showing me Sleepy Hollow."

"Hey, no problem. And thanks for the shades. The name alone will always make me think of you."

"Cool."

"Bonza." He remains at the door.

"See ya," I say quietly.

And then he is kissing me. Not in an overpowering way but just softly and gently—on the mouth. And then he straightens up and it's over. I look up at him and despite my Billabong sunnies, I am certain I see stars.

"See ya," he says, then picks up his board and walks over to his car.

Somehow I manage to turn on the ignition and wave as I pull out of the parking lot. But I feel like I'm flying. *Just get home safely*, I tell myself, *no bungles on the highway.*

And somehow I do. But for the life of me I can't remember the trip. Can't remember taking the exits, changing lanes, staying on the right side of the road. But here I am in Uncle Ron's garage and the Jeep is still in one piece. And so am I, but I feel like I'm walking on clouds.

"What are you so happy about?" asks Vanessa when I go inside. She is in her favorite veg-out position: on the leather sectional, remote in hand, flipping endlessly through the channels.

"You really want to know?"

She sits up and pats the seat beside her. "Yeah, tell me everything."

And so I do. Oh, I don't mention that I'm the one who bought the matching sunnies. Somehow that seems as if it would tarnish my story a bit. Although I like to think of myself as a "liberated" woman, as my mom puts it. But I think I'm a bit old-fashioned when it comes to romance. Not that I'm an expert. Ha! The honest truth is that Wyatt is only the second guy to kiss me.

The first one was Caleb Milligan back in PNG. Caleb is a class ahead of me, and we went steady for a couple of months last year. I'm not even sure why. Probably because other kids were pairing off, and it seemed like the thing to do. But "going steady" in a mission school consists of walking together without holding hands or any public show of affection, although kids have been known to sneak around and give private unmentionable displays of affection. And although her family still denies it, we all know that Rebecca Witherspoon got pregnant last January, and that's why she got shipped back home to Sydney. But when Caleb Milligen kissed me, I never saw stars. I never walked on clouds.

"Do you think he could be the one?" I ask Vanessa.

She considers this. "Maybe. I think that Bryce could be the one for me. But we're awfully young to know these things for sure. I do know that I like Bryce's family."

"You mean his money?"

She shrugs. "It's part of the package."

"Would you marry someone for money, Vanessa?"

"Not money alone. I'd have to love him too."

"But what if you fell in love with someone poor? Would you marry him?"

Her face scrunches together as if she's really considering this. "I don't think I could fall in love with someone who was poor."

"Oh."

"Now, that doesn't mean you shouldn't fall in love with Wyatt, Hannah. And even though he's a bit hard up for money these days, his family is good for it. And he's worth getting involved with."

I nod. But what I was really wondering was whether Wyatt would want to get involved with someone poor like me. Then again, why should he know that I'm poor? Maybe he assumes since I'm Vanessa's cousin and dress like the other wealthy kids, I must be rich too. Or maybe it doesn't matter. That's what I prefer to think. I reckon that Wyatt's like me, accepting people for who they are. That's why he wasn't troubled about being with me and Jessie. We're certainly not in the "in" crowd. And yet Wyatt doesn't seem to mind.

It's not until I go upstairs that I realize I left my beach bag and clothes in Wyatt's car. I wonder if he's noticed yet or if I should call him. It's not that I really need those things, although that is one of my best outfits and there are things I'd like from my beach bag. I decide to let it ride until after dinner. Then, just as I'm helping Aunt Lori load the dishwasher, the phone rings. It's Wyatt.

"I noticed you left your things in my car," he says. "Want me to drop them by?"

"Would you mind?"

"Not a bit." He tells me he knows where Vanessa lives and that he'll be by in about twenty minutes.

"A boyfriend?" asks Aunt Lori with raised brows.

"Maybe."

"Ooh, fun. You're not even here a full month, and you've already got a boyfriend. Who is he?" I tell her, and she thinks that's great. "Wyatt seems like a nice kid. And not hard on the eyes either."

"Right." I turn and glance at the clock. "Maybe I should scrub up a bit before he rocks up."

She nods. "I would."

So I pop upstairs and after a quick rummage through my closet, which seems sparser than usual, I decide on my Diesel jeans (which Vanessa lusts over but can't squeeze into). And after trying several tops, I settle on the turquoise DKNY tank, which really makes me look tan. I put on my Prada belt and sandals and then go downstairs trying to act cool and casual.

"I hear Wyatt's coming over," says Vanessa in a singsong voice.

"Just to drop some stuff by," I tell her. "I forgot my work clothes in the back of his car."

Vanessa is walking with her arms crossed and nodding as if she's just discovered some big secret. "You left some clothes in the back of his car? Very interesting, Hannah. What's up with that?"

I pick up a pillow and toss it at her. "Very funny. That's not how it was at all." So I explain how I changed into my bathers at Mac's and needed a place to stow my clothes.

"Yeah, yeah, whatever."

"It's true."

"I know, Hannah. I'm just jerking your chain."

"Jerking my chain . . ." I nod, considering this new slang. "Yes, that's rather what it feels like."

Then he's at the door, and I'm desperately hoping that Vanessa won't make innuendos in front of Wyatt.

"Here you go," he says, holding out my things.

"Thanks so much. Do you want to come in? Have a soda or something?"

"Sounds good."

So I lead him into the house, and thankfully Vanessa has vanished, although she could be lurking about somewhere listening. I set my clothes on a bench by the stairway, go to the fridge, and list off the choices of soda. I can feel Wyatt standing behind me now and know that he can easily see Uncle Ron's beers in there. I'm sure that he'd be interested, but there's no way I'm going to do something that stupid.

"Pepsi sounds good," he finally says.

So I take out two Pepsis, even though I don't especially care for the stuff, and set them on the counter. "Do you want a glass and ice?"

"Sure."

So I find two glasses, fill them with the miraculous ice that falls right out of the fridge door, and take them over to the counter.

"Got any lemon?" he asks.

"Lemon?"

"Yeah, lemon is good with Pepsi. Haven't you tried it?"

I shake my head and go back for lemon. Thankfully, Aunt Lori keeps them sliced and in one of those bags that fasten on top.

I drop one in each glass. "Want to go out by the pool?"

"Sounds good."

And I lead him outside. For some reason I feel more at ease out here. Maybe it's because of the way I grew up, being outdoors most of the time. I walk over to the table and chairs on the far side of the pool, knowing that it's unlikely Vanessa can hear us over here. Not that I have anything to hide. But for some reason I want this conversation to remain private. At least until I report back to her, which I'm certain to do before the night is over.

Mostly we just yabber about nothing much. But it feels like a flirty kind of conversation, like we're trying to find out about each other and yet don't want to reveal too much or anything that would put the anchors down. Finally it's starting to get dark, and I shift in my chair, almost as if I'm getting up, although I'm not.

"I should go," he says suddenly. "I know you have to get up early for work."

"Well, yeah," I admit. Then I walk him through the side yard and through the gate that leads to the front of the house.

"So I'll pick you up around seven thirty tomorrow?" he says.

"Sure, that sounds great."

We're at his car now. And I'm just standing there, knowing I should say good night and go inside, but it's like my sandals are cemented to the driveway. He puts his hands on my shoulders now. "You're really special, Hannah," he says in a quiet voice. Then he leans down and kisses me again. This time I make sure that he knows I'm kissing him back, and we stand there for what feels like seconds but might be minutes before we stop.

Then he takes in a breath and smiles. "See you tomorrow."

I nod. "See ya."

And once again I'm walking on clouds.

seventeen

AFTER I GET HOME FROM WORK ON FRIDAY, I SPEND MOST OF THE afternoon just getting ready for the big party. But it's not as much fun as I thought it would be. The truth is, I am getting really worried about the expensive outfit I'm wearing, wondering why in the world I spent more than $1,000 for just one evening. I even go to the wastebasket in my bathroom, thinking I might find the tags and return the clothing tomorrow, but Consuela has already tidied up in there, and the trash is gone. Just to be on the safe side, I put on some extra antiperspirant. I don't want to ruin this expensive top!

Then while I'm waiting for Wyatt to show up, I start feeling seriously worried. And it's only partly about Wyatt. Oh, I reckon it's possible he's forgotten me or gone back to Felicia or been eaten by sharks while surfing some lonely beach this afternoon. But Wyatt's lateness isn't the only thing that's eating me.

It all started when I picked up my paycheck after lunch break today. I had already done the math in my head, multiplying my hourly wage times the hours I've worked. And while I didn't plan to get rich, I thought at least I could start getting out of debt and have a bit of spending money, although I still wouldn't have any extra for school. But when I opened the envelope and looked at the amount on the check, I nearly screamed.

At first I thought there was some mistake. It couldn't possibly be true. Then I looked at the slip of paper stapled to my check, some sort of bookkeeping thing I think, and it seemed that a fair amount of money had been subtracted from the total of what I should've been paid. I asked Carlita about this since she works in the accounting department. "Do you think it's possible that someone made an error on my paycheck?"

She gave me this you-poor-daft-Sheila kind of smile. "There's a little something you may not be aware of," she said, "seeing you live in another country and all. But here in the good old U.S. of A., we pay *taxes*. Uncle Sam gets his due before we get ours. It's the American way, sweetheart. Get used to it."

Consequently, my two-week check, minus federal and state taxes and other various deductions, is barely enough to cover the $500 every other week that I promised to pay Uncle Ron for the draw he gave me from his own personal account. And then I discovered, also through Carlita, that my Macy's charge account (which I'm only able to make the minimum payment on) is going to start accumulating interest—every day until the entire amount is paid off in full. *Gulp!*

It's nearly eight when I finally see Wyatt pull up. I realize he's only thirty minutes late, but that was thirty minutes of obsessing and worrying that I could've done without. Even so, I try to act cool and laid back, but inside I'm a complete mess.

I open the door and there is Wyatt with a big grin on his face. But does he apologize or even give any excuse for being late? Of course not.

"Hey, babe," he says as he gives me a hug and then a kiss. "You look fantastic!" And of course, all my ill feelings are wiped neatly away.

"Thanks." I walk ahead of him toward the passenger door, taking my time so that he can take me in.

"Seriously, Hannah, you look totally awesome." Then he pauses and really checks me out. "But what happened to my little Aussie surfer girl?"

I frown and hold out my hands. "You mean you don't like this?"

"No, not at all. I think you look way cool, babe. Totally amazing." He opens the passenger door and waits as I get in. "I'm just glad to know there's a surfer chick underneath all that glamour."

I smile up at him. "Been surfing today?"

"As a matter of fact . . ." Then he closes the door and runs around to the other side and gets in. "Man, the waves were so rad today, I could hardly tear myself away from the beach. You should've been there, Hannah."

"Wish I had been."

Then he tells me about the place he went to and who was there and how the waves were "treacherous."

"You mean it was dangerous?"

"No, just killer, you know. Great tides. Really huge waves. Think it has to do with the moon or something, but let me tell you, it was awesome."

I'm amazed at how long this guy can go on and on, just talking about surfing. Not that I mind since I've been enjoying it too. I'm just amazed. And I'm glad we share this interest. I just hope it's not the only thing we both enjoy together. Well, surfing and kissing. And I guess I should be glad that he's so talkative since nearly all I do while we drive is listen. But the way Wyatt talks, you'd think he'd like to spend his entire life on a board.

"You really love to surf, don't you?"

"There's nothing else like it." Then he laughs. "Well, almost nothing else."

"I'm surprised you're going to school on the East Coast."

He exhales loudly and shakes his head. "It's not exactly my first choice."

"Why's that?"

Then he goes on to tell me how the only way he can stay in his dad's "good graces"—which basically ensures Wyatt money—is to attend his dad's alma mater. "I'd never go there otherwise."

"Oh."

"Sometimes I think I might bail on him anyway. Oh, I'll give his school a try, but if it's as bad as I think it will be, hey, I might just go AWOL or something. Come back and turn into a real beach bum. Maybe travel around the world, surfing all the best spots."

"What will your major be in college?" I feel pleased that I remembered the word *major* since I only just learned it from Uncle Ron.

"I haven't got a clue." He shrugs and turns toward what I am thinking is the Hollywood area, although I'm still pretty unfamiliar with this place.

"Well, what do you like doing?" I persist.

"Surfing."

I laugh. "Too bad they don't let you major in that."

"Yeah."

Then we both get quiet, and I suspect that I'm pulling him down with all this talk about uni. "Where's the party at?" I ask suddenly, hoping to change the subject. "I know that Vanessa's been helping Bryce with it, but I don't recall if she said where it's at."

"It's at Bryce's grandma's house. She has this cool old place in Beverly Hills. Bryce doesn't live with her, but it sounds like she lets him do pretty much what he likes there. As long as he doesn't make too much noise or disturb her. But she's half-deaf anyway, so it's usually no problem. She just stays in her room while Bryce throws the raddest parties."

"Beverly Hills," I say with a bit of awe. "I can't imagine ever being so rich that I could afford a house in Beverly Hills. Vanessa took me on a little driving tour and showed me where some of your Hollywood celebs live. Pretty impressive."

"It's okay, but Beverly Hills isn't the greatest place to live. Give me a place in Malibu or Laguna, and I'd be happy any day."

"You mean a place with a beach?" I tease.

"You got that right."

Soon he is turning into a driveway that's flanked by open iron gates. We drive around behind the house, where there are at least a dozen cars parked already. Some I recognize. I smooth my skirt with my palms, I'm not even sure why—maybe just bracing myself. I'm sure Felicia will be here tonight. In some ways I feel a bit like the lamb being led to the slaughter, or maybe the fatted calf, because I know that Vanessa is out to get back at Felicia through me tonight. But what if her plan backfires? What if it's Felicia who comes out on top?

Wyatt turns off the car and looks at me. "You nervous?"

I shrug. "A bit, I guess. I've heard that Felicia isn't, well . . ."

"Felicia is history," he says quickly. "As far as I'm concerned anyway."

"What if she doesn't feel the same way about you?"

He laughs. "From what I heard, she's already working on a new guy."

"Alright then." I take in a deep breath. "Just breathe, right? Like I'm about to ride the big one in?"

He laughs. "Hey, I like your style!" Then he helps me out of the car and takes me by the hand. "And like I said earlier, you look really great, Hannah. You'll be the prettiest girl here."

And naturally, that makes me smile. So we both enter smiling and happy, and the first person I see—across the room by the open french doors—is Felicia. And she doesn't look happy to see us.

But in the next instant, she is smiling and coming directly toward us. "Hey, Hannah," she says sweetly, even giving me the kiss-on-both-cheeks thing that she and her friends do to each other. Does this mean I'm a member of the club? "Good to see you." Then she steps back and looks at my outfit, her brows rising with . . . could it be appreciation? "You look absolutely gorgeous, girl. Is that Iceberg?"

I nod. "Yeah, thanks." I suppress the urge to tell her that I just got it, especially for this party. Vanessa has made it clear that too much talk focused specifically on money or clothes makes it sound like you're trying too hard. "It has to look easy," she keeps telling me. "You look great too," I tell Felicia. "But then, you always look amazing."

She smiles again, and I can't tell, but I think it may be partially sincere. "Why, thank you." Then she turns to Wyatt and says, "It looks like you took my advice."

"Advice?" He looks wary.

"About hooking up with Hannah. Why, this girl's got it all. She's a surfer chick and knows her way around fashion. How much better could you do?"

Now Wyatt smiles as if he's relieved, but I think I hear sarcasm in her tone. Even so, I keep smiling.

"There you are," says Vanessa, moving toward me. "I wondered if you two would ever get here. We're expecting Clayton any second.

The plan is to hide out by the pool and then yell *surprise*."

"And such a clever plan it is," says Felicia. Then she goes over to greet someone else.

I feel Wyatt's arm slipping around my waist, and I suspect he's thinking that we're home free. But I'm thinking the party hasn't even begun.

Bryce and Vanessa are shooing us all outside now. And to keep Clayton off track, all the lights are out. The sun is just going down. Wyatt and I go off to a corner where he slips both arms around me and pulls me toward him for a little kiss. But I feel uncomfortable. It must be all those years of mission-school rules. Anyway, I pull away.

"What's wrong, babe?"

I shrug. "Nothing. I just thought I heard someone saying that Clayton was coming." And then, to my great relief, Clayton is coming and we're all yelling "Surprise!" and "Happy birthday!" and people are going forward and congratulating him. And Wyatt and I get rather swallowed up by the crowd. Soon the lights and music come on, and people start eating and drinking and loosening up. Even though I really don't want it, I take the wine cooler that Wyatt brings me. I'd much rather have a soft drink. But I sip at it and look around at the people. As always, everyone looks nice—make that *expensive*—and I realize that if it weren't for my clothes, I would not feel like I fit in at all. Even now, I'm not so sure.

"Where did you get that outfit?" Elisa is suddenly asking me. "It's so great on you."

So I tell her, briefly, then add, "Vanessa helped me pick it out."

Elisa winks at me as if she already knows. "Well, you look absolutely amazing in it."

"You're looking quite chic yourself," I say. "But I've never seen you not."

"Oh, you're just being sweet."

"No, I love your style."

She hooks her arm into mine now. "Well, I'm going to have to adopt you as my new best friend, Hannah. You think Vanessa will mind?"

I know she's kidding, but my discomfort only increases as she takes me around, introducing me to people I haven't met. I wonder if this is something that she and Vanessa set up to get at Felicia. Mostly it's just making my head hurt, and I know I'll never remember all these names.

"Oh, you're that cute little Aussie girl who was surfing with Wyatt," says a pretty Asian girl with short hair. "I wish I knew how to surf."

"You should learn," I tell her. "It's really fun."

"But I've heard you can get really bruised up. My brother even knocked a tooth out while he was trying to learn. And then there are the sharks." She gives a dramatic shudder.

"Hey, babe," says Wyatt from behind me. "Where'd you run off to?"

Elisa smiles at him. "I was just introducing her around. I guess you can have her back now."

So we go sit over by some of Wyatt's friends, and before I know it, Wyatt has brought me another wine cooler, even though I haven't finished the first one. "I'm alright," I tell him. "I think I'll just have a soft drink next go 'round."

"Just want you to have fun, babe."

Then I sit and listen as Wyatt replays to his buddies how "epic" the surfing was today. I try to appear interested, but I've heard this surf report once already. Finally I excuse myself to the ladies' room and go inside the house. The truth is, I actually do need to go. I ask

Vanessa (who is acting uncharacteristically domestic as she arranges crackers and cheese on a silver tray) for directions, and she points me to one of the closest guest-bedroom suites. "It's lots roomier than the powder room," she tells me. So I follow her directions and head down the hallway.

This is one of the oldest homes I've been in since coming to the States. I reckon this house might be nearly one hundred years old. And quite glamorous. I heard that some old movie star built it back when films were just beginning. I remind myself to try to find out more. The bedroom is rather splendid with its gilt furniture and silky bedspread and large mirrors everywhere. I go through it until I come to the bathroom in back, then close and lock the door. I take my time in the bathroom, allowing myself to really admire all the old fixtures and marble and whatnot. And then I hear female voices outside the door. Thinking someone is waiting, I'm about to go out when I hear, "That Hannah is so totally lame!" and then laughter.

I pause with my hand on the gold doorknob, waiting for more.

"She thinks she's so hot, like she can just waltz in here and take Wyatt," says a voice that sounds exactly like Felicia's.

That's when I notice a keyhole above the ornate doorknob. I bend down to look through and see that it is Felicia. Along with Bree and Elisa. Now, I'm not surprised to see Bree, but I thought Elisa was on our side. Not that we have sides. They're primping in front of one of the big mirrors.

"Wyatt's only into her because of the surfing thing," Elisa says to Felicia. "Vanessa told me so."

"How does Vanessa know?" asks Felicia.

"She's Hannah's cousin," says Bree.

"I know *that*," snaps Felicia. "I mean how does Vanessa know what Wyatt's interested in?"

Now I'm wondering if this isn't some kind of setup for Felicia. Maybe Elisa is working as a double agent. So I just continue to listen and watch through my peephole.

"Well, everyone knows that Hannah is . . . well, she's *not* one of us," continues Elisa. "I mean, you should've seen her when she got here. Her hair was this mousy brown with a horrible cut, and she wore these awful clothes that looked like she'd found them in some homeless shelter."

More laughter.

"And her parents are missionaries!" says Felicia as if this is as funny as being clowns in a circus. "I just learned that delectable bit of news from Jessie. Of course, Jessie thinks that's a positive. But then you guys know what a freak Jessie is. I think she'd like to become a missionary herself."

Now the laughter is absolutely grating.

"Seriously, Felicia," says Elisa. "Don't worry about her. I don't think she has a chance with Wyatt."

"No one can compete with you, Felice," says Bree in a way that makes me think that Bree might as well bend over and lick Felicia's pretty Prada sandals.

"Well, if Hannah the missionary thinks she can get into this crowd with the purchase of one measly Iceberg outfit, she better think again."

"It was a nice outfit," says Bree meekly.

"It makes her butt look big," says Elisa.

"And that color . . ." Felicia makes a face into the mirror. "Well, it's okay for my grandmother."

"And Hannah," adds Elisa, a bit too vindictively I think. I'm rethinking the whole double agent thing.

They all laugh.

"But I don't get it," says Bree. "I thought you and Vanessa were friends. Why are you standing up for Felicia all of a sudden?"

"Elisa and I were friends way back in grade school, weren't we?" Felicia is putting her arm protectively around Elisa now.

"Vanessa's been more like a project than a friend," says Elisa. "I mean, her dad runs a cleaning business, *puh-leez!* And she had absolutely no fashion sense when they first moved here. I guess I felt sorry for her and decided to be like Pygmalion for her." She laughs now as if this is really funny.

"Like in that old movie *Clueless*?" asks Bree.

"That's such a lame movie."

"Well, you did a good job with her anyway," says Bree. And although I'm liking this girl more, I'm also thinking she's pretty clueless herself.

"A good job?" says Felicia hotly. "A good job?" Then she turns to Elisa. "No offense, but Vanessa is a loser. Anyone can see it. First of all, her dad runs a janitorial service—I mean, he cleans toilets for a living, for pete's sake! Second of all, Vanessa is totally hopeless. I mean, not only is she fat, but she's boring. And the way she gloms on to people just because they have money. It makes me sick. Like Bryce, for instance. You think she really sees anything in that nerdster?"

"I kind of like Bryce," says Bree in a meek voice.

"Well, that just figures." Felicia turns back to Elisa. "But, seriously, don't be offended, Elisa. You did your best with Vanessa. You took the poor girl as far as she could go. She just doesn't have it. Honestly, I'd have more hope for that hokey Hannah the missionary than Vanessa. At least she's not fat—"

And that's all I can take. I burst out the door and just stare at the three of them. "That's enough!" I say when I've recovered enough to speak. "You three girls should be ashamed of yourselves talking about a mate like that. You are nothing but a bunch of superficial, self-centered, dimwitted snobs. And Vanessa is way better off without the whole lot of you. I know that I'm ready to be rid of you. Why I ever tried to be part of this lamebrain crowd is way beyond me!" Then I stomp out of the room, go straight to Wyatt, and tell him I want to leave.

eighteen

It doesn't take long to find Wyatt. He's still sitting with his mates, still chugging down beers, and still regaling them with tales of adventures in surfing.

"I want to go home," I tell him.

"But the party's just starting," he complains.

"Fine. Stay if you like, but I'm going. I don't care if I have to call a cab."

"What's wrong, babe?" He's on his feet now and escorting me to what I'm sure he thinks is a quieter corner.

I give him the short version of what I just heard, and he starts to laugh. "What's so funny?" I demand.

"Chicks. They're just like that."

"I'm not like that."

"Well, you're different, Hannah."

"That's right. And I have no desire to be a part of this crowd." By now I can see the vicious trio emerging. You could never tell by their faces that I'd just given them what for. But why should that surprise me? These girls are so cool you could make Popsicles up their backsides!

"Just chill," he tells me. "This, whatever it is, will blow over."

"I'm not going to chill. I'm gonna get going."

And then I walk away. I have no idea whether he is coming or not. And I'm not sure that I care. I stop by Vanessa, who's still working in the kitchen. "Sorry, cuz, but I'm leaving early."

"You're leaving?" She looks dismayed, and it's all I can do not to reach out and hug her and tell her to run while she can. But I don't. This is Vanessa's crowd. She probably knows them better than I do. "Is Wyatt taking you home?"

I shrug. "I don't know and I don't care."

"Did you guys have a fight?"

"Not really. I'm, uh, I just want to go is all." I can tell by now that Wyatt is probably not coming. "I think I'll call a cab."

"No, don't do that," says Vanessa. "Why don't you take my car? I'll have Bryce run me home later."

"You sure?"

She nods and jots down some basic directions to get me back to the right freeway. "Just take care."

"No worries," I tell her. "You do the same."

"My keys are in my purse, and that's back in the second bedroom on the left down the hallway."

"Thanks." So once again, I head down the hallway. I'm feeling slightly less furious than I was earlier, but I'm still about as mad as a cut snake. I can't get those girls' words out of my head. I go into what I assume is the right bedroom, a very opulent-looking room full of rugs and antiques and art objects. But something's not right. And I can hear this sniffling sound. I peer across the dimly lit room to see a small figure sitting in a plush red chair. There, with tears streaming down her face, sits an ancient-looking, white-haired lady. I can't help but notice her jewelry, and I wonder if she served as inspiration for the phrase "dripping in diamonds."

"Please excuse me," I say quickly, realizing I must've walked in on Bryce's grandmother. "I must've gotten the wrong room. I didn't mean to disturb you."

"Please leave," she commands me in a shaky voice.

"Yes," I say, nervously backing up. "I'm terribly sorry." I consider asking her what's wrong, but her icy expression is too intimidating. It seems obvious that she's not interested in my companionship. Even so, I feel sorry for her. She seems extremely unhappy. As I locate the right bedroom, not nearly as ritzy as the suite Bryce's grandmother occupies, I can't shake the image of that old woman from my head. The thought of her sitting there in complete misery amid her accumulation of wealth and riches is rather disturbing.

I find Vanessa's purse and remove her keys, then retrace my steps through this maze of a house, careful not to walk in on Bryce's grandma again. I hear the voices of partiers down the hall, including Elisa's. I still feel a bit confused about that girl. At first I really believed she was putting on an act. After all, she's been quite nice to me, generally speaking, even taking me about and introducing me to her mates tonight. But when she spewed out all that nonsense about how she'd played Pygmalion to Vanessa, recreating her so she'd be fit for society—the society of a bunch of dogs—it made me feel sick.

I drive Vanessa's beautiful car with the top down through this glamorous neighborhood, me dressed in my designer clothes, and I don't feel the least bit impressive. Even when some blokes honk their horn, waving and whistling at me, I still feel like a total loser. Not so much because of what happened tonight. Felicia and her mates aren't worth feeling bad over. I feel rotten because I am seeing myself as I really am.

Despite whatever image I think I may have created or am possibly projecting, I feel more lost and pitiful than ever before. Worse than this, I feel like I've been shafted. But I reckon it's my own fault.

And my worries about debt and money make me feel like I can barely breathe. I am fully aware that I am going in the hole and going fast! After seeing today's paycheck and doing the arithmetic, I realized that by the end of the summer, I will have nothing whatsoever saved for uni or a trip to Dallas to see my brothers or anything else for that matter, and I may have to get a second job just to pay for this stupid designer outfit I'm wearing tonight.

And all for what? How did I get myself into this bungle? And why? I feel like the biggest loser in the entire civilized world—make that uncivilized too because the people in our village back in New Guinea would never be this stupid. I should've known better than to fall into an idiot trap like this. What on earth is wrong with me?

And I have to wonder while I'm at it if I would have ended up in this hopeless hole if I hadn't pushed God out of my life. Maybe Jessie was right. Is this my just reward for turning my back on him? If it is, I just might want to give up completely. Why bother? Why don't I just drive Vanessa's beautiful car over a cliff? I happen to know where a good one is on the way to the VanHorn's beach house. But with my luck I'd emerge without a single bruise, her car would be ruined, and then I'd owe even more money for that.

So I keep driving as if everything is fine. Anyone who sees me right now probably assumes that my life is just as perfect on the inside as it appears to be on the outside. Young, rich girl driving gorgeous car—doesn't she have it good? I find myself looking at other beautiful people driving their expensive vehicles and wearing their designer clothes and their fool's gold bling bling—people who, like me, seem to have it all together. And suddenly I'm wondering, *Do they really have it all together? Or are they (like me and most everyone else I know) just fooling themselves?*

nineteen

I FEEL AS IF SOMETHING IN ME IS DEAD OR MAYBE JUST DYING. THE OLD Hannah seems as far off as Papua New Guinea. Just a memory perhaps. It's been nearly a fortnight since that fateful party at Bryce's grandma's house. But I feel as if I've turned into a different person since then—or perhaps simply a nonperson.

Vanessa is completely fed up with me. "All you do is work and sulk," she's said on a regular basis for days now. "Can't you see that Wyatt's not worth it?" Or she'll say, "You should get out and have some fun." She always ends with, "I know what'll cheer you up. We should go shopping!"

Shopping? I keep myself from overreacting as I calmly explain to her that I cannot afford to go shopping. And then she just gets aggravated. But she's right about one thing: All I do is work. As far as the sulking goes, that's not really fair. I reckon it looks like sulking to her, but the fact is, I don't have the energy to do anything else. Maybe that's why I feel dead. I've been putting in ten-hour days for nearly two weeks, and as a result, I'm completely zonked.

Cynthia had said some people were taking vacations in July, and she needed to hire some temporary help. So I talked her into letting me work some extra hours. "Just for a few weeks?" I pleaded.

"Is your uncle okay with this?" she asked with skepticism.

"I'm sure he'll be fine." And after I talked to him about it, convincing him it was only for a little while, he agreed.

But Cynthia was on to me, and one day she invited me to have lunch with her. "Are you in over your head, Hannah?"

"What do you mean?"

"I mean financially. It's not that unusual. Lots of girls get caught up in the spending game, running up credit cards until it looks like they'll never catch up. I even fell into that trap myself when I was in my twenties."

"Really?" Now, this took me by surprise. Cynthia seems like such a sensible person, so grounded and even-keeled.

She sighed heavily, almost as if she didn't want to remember. "I'd just gotten out of college. I had my first real job, and all the women there dressed so nicely that I felt really out of place. I got my first credit card so I could buy a few things to help me fit in." She shook her head. "And then I got another credit card, and before long I had several and they were all maxed out."

"Right," I said, not liking where this was going.

"But I was in some kind of denial. I thought that I'd be able to get them all paid off before long. But between paying for rent and utilities and my car and everything else, I could never make more than the minimum payment, and the bills just kept getting bigger and bigger."

"So what did you do?" I'm sure my voice sounded as flat and hopeless as I felt.

"I had to get a financial counselor. She put me on a really strict budget and taught me how to cut corners and put more money toward my monthly payments. It took about seven years, but I finally got out from under it."

Seven years? No way! Seven years sounded like a lifetime or a prison sentence. But I thanked her for sharing her story and pretended to have been encouraged by it, though I actually wanted to be sick right there in the little café.

But her story has helped motivate me to stick to my get-out-of-debt plan. Oh, sure, I may be drained from my long days in the dreary office. I get up before dawn, get off work at five, and drive home during rush hour, which makes my commute even longer. I eat a bit of dinner and fall into bed exhausted. I don't even swim in the pool anymore. And my tan has faded to a sallow gray. I haven't surfed in a fortnight. I feel like an indentured servant. We learned about them in Australian history—impoverished people who sold themselves for a period of time to pay off their family's debts, just a step above a slave. Only these debts are my own.

These feelings are driven home even more soundly as I observe Vanessa and her friends still running around, enjoying their leisure time, going to parties, dating their boyfriends, and shopping, shopping, shopping. I try not to watch.

I never did tell Vanessa what her mates said about her that night at the party. Somehow it didn't seem my place. And strangely enough they have all treated her exactly the same as before, maybe even better. She seems happier than ever being with girls like Elisa and Felicia. I suspect they got worried about their social faux pas and are relieved that I've not only kept my mouth shut but pulled off a remarkable disappearing act to boot.

Wyatt called a couple of times during the weekend following the party, leaving rather ambiguous messages on my cell phone, mostly wanting to know if I wanted to go surfing. But nothing specific and no apologies. I never called him back. Why should I?

It was only a matter of days before he and Felicia were back together again anyway. Big surprise there. Vanessa was right: Felicia gets what Felicia wants. For that matter, maybe Wyatt does too. A broke bloke like him needs someone with deep pockets. Not only that, but he has a private beach to surf on and sailing trips on the weekends too. He must think he's in surfer-dude heaven.

Jessie called a couple of times, leaving messages that I likewise ignored. But then I began to feel guilty. After all, Jessie isn't like the others. So after a couple of days, I called her back but only got her messaging service. I simply told her that I'm working long days for a while and that I'd let her know when life returned to normal. Normal? What is that? Normal here in the States seems to involve a lifestyle I can't keep up with. Even though I was tired last night, I stayed up long enough to watch one of Vanessa's favorite shows, *What Not to Wear*. I found myself, not for the first time, wishing that I was the lucky victim they picked to be on their show. But if it were me and they handed me that Visa card worth $5,000, I would just run. I'd take it to the bank and use it to pay off all my debt. Of course, that would be breaking "the rules." But as I watched this woman spend her five grand on not that many items of clothing, I had to wonder, *How is she going to keep this up when she goes home? Is she going to get her own Visa card and max it out? And then what? What is wrong with this picture?*

"Want to go to the big sale at Macy's today?" Laticia asked me a few days ago.

"No thanks." I produced the fake smile that comes more and more easily.

And then yesterday, "There's a one-day sale today," Carlita told me enticingly. "All their summer things are on clearance—even designer clothes."

"No thanks." Again with the smile.

I don't try to explain my refusal to do anything with anyone. It's just easier this way. And, I assure myself, this is only a temporary situation. Still, I'm not so sure. I feel like I've been locked away in debtor's prison. Of course, it's my own creation. Still, I worry I might lose the keys. Perhaps I've already lost them.

Finally it's the weekend after my second payday, and I almost feel as if I can breathe again. I'm not sure if the nightmares will go away yet, the ones where I am thrown into jail for unpaid bills or sold as a slave to pay off my debts. There's also one where I'm at a fancy party wearing my fancy clothes, and the other girls start tearing them off me, piece by piece, saying, "You never paid for those things; they don't belong to you." And then I am standing there naked and humiliated while everyone looks on and laughs.

Maybe I need therapy. Yanks are big on therapy.

But maybe the dreams will lighten up a bit now. I can only hope. The first thing I did after depositing my check in the bank was go straight to Macy's, where I paid off nearly half of what I owe that store. Then I wrote a check to my uncle, which means I've paid off half of what I owe him as well. And I still have a bit left to tide me over until my next paycheck. Even so, I keep reminding myself that I must continue to live like a church mouse or, even better, a missionary! We missionaries know how to be frugal. My mum reminded me of that during her last phone call.

"We've been camping out," she told me.

"Camping out?"

"Yes, we got a mattress that just fits in the back of the station wagon. And we've had a great time visiting some state parks. Your dad bought a little charcoal barbie, and we've had some lovely meals. And think of the money we've saved!"

"Sounds like fun," I said in a voice that sounded unconvincing.

"Well, it's nothing like the luxuries you're enjoying with our rich relatives, but it's good enough for Dad and me. We're used to roughing it."

"I know, Mum." And as I reconsidered my initial reaction, I decided that camping in the back of a car with no worries and no bills could actually be more fun than the way I'm living now. But I didn't say this. I didn't say anything to clue my mum off to the kind of financial difficulties I've gotten myself into. I knew my practical mum would never understand such incredible stupidity.

"Now, don't you get too spoiled there," my mum warned. "We don't want you to be impossible to live with when we pick you up at the end of August."

"No worries," I assured her. If only she knew. But thank goodness she doesn't.

"Don't you want to go shopping with me today?" begs Vanessa when she discovers me out by the pool trying to revive a bit of my faded tan.

"No thanks." I give her my standard reply without even opening my eyes.

"You are absolutely no fun, Hannah." She flops down in the chaise beside me with a loud *harrumph*. "It's been two weeks since this business with Wyatt. You can't possibly be —"

"It's not about Wyatt." I sit up and consider leaping into the pool. It would be the first time I've gone swimming in a fortnight.

"Then what is it about?" She turns on her side and studies me with interest.

Now I consider telling her my woes. So far I've kept my humiliating financial secrets to myself, but maybe I owe Vanessa an explanation. And so I tell her the short version of what I've gone through.

"Is *that* all?" she says, actually laughing.

I don't know what I expected, but certainly not such casual

nonchalance or dismissal. A bit of sympathy would've been nice, or even a speck of respect. "Sorry, but it's been a pretty big thing to me," I say defensively. "The reason I took that job was to put aside some money for uni. But all I did was go deeper and deeper into debt. It was making me crazy. I'm only just starting to feel a bit of relief now, and I'm only halfway out. But I'm also totally wrecked from all the work."

"Well, if it makes you feel any better, Dad has been getting on me about my credit card bills. He's actually putting me on a budget."

"Truly?" I attempt a sympathetic expression.

She frowns. "Yes, and it's not fair. All my friends spend way more money than I do. How can I possibly keep up?"

I sigh. "This whole *keeping up* bit is ludicrous, crazy, ridiculous!"

She nods sadly, almost as if the reality of that is sinking in. "Yeah, I sort of agree with you."

"Then why don't you stop?"

"Because I can't, Hannah." Now she smiles, a bit slyly it seems. "Or maybe I don't want to."

"But you admitted it was crazy—"

"A good kind of crazy." Now she lowers her voice as if making a true confession. "You know what, Hannah? *I think I may be a shopping addict.* I saw a special on Oprah once. All these women were on who have closets full of things they never use, lots with tags still on or still in the bags—people who just spend and spend and spend, spendaholics, shopping addicts, whatever you want to call them. But I'm not alone. I think my friends are addicted to shopping too. I think we all are."

"I'm not."

"You've come close, Hannah. I saw the look in your eyes that day we got the Iceberg outfit. You were so happy."

197

"I was not *happy*." I consider this, wanting to be honest and yet not sure that I even know how to explain it. "It was another feeling . . . it's hard to explain. But I was *not* happy."

"Whatever. You were having a good time."

"But it was a *false* sense of a good time, Vanessa. Like if you take a drug to feel good, but then it wears off, and you feel worse than ever. The shopping high went away too, and then I got stuck with the bill. And after that I got depressed." I don't tell her that I'm still depressed and may continue being depressed forever since it seems this dark cloud may never go away.

She doesn't say anything, and I'm wondering if maybe she really does know how I feel. Maybe she's experiencing some of these same feelings too. I heard Aunt Lori once use the term "buyer's remorse." Is it possible that I'm not alone here?

"You know, Vanessa, if I could take all those expensive clothes and shoes and everything back, I would," I continue. "I only wore that Iceberg outfit once. I don't ever want to wear it again. I don't even want to look at it. I want to chunder every time I see it because it reminds me of how stupid I was."

"That's silly, Hannah. You looked fantastic in that—" But she is interrupted by her phone ringing. She answers quickly to escape this conversation, I suspect. And I can tell by her answer that it's Elisa (the "friend" who took on Vanessa as her "project"), and it sounds as if they're going to go . . . *shopping*.

"Sure you don't want to come?" asks Vanessa with her sweetest smile. "I promise I won't pressure you to buy anything."

"Better to avoid the temptation altogether," I say.

"But Mom's going to bug me about leaving you home all by yourself again."

"Maybe I'll call Jessie." I say, thinking I probably won't. The truth is, I still don't really want to talk to or see anyone.

"That's a great idea," says Vanessa. "You should call Jessie. You and she seemed to hit it off right from the start. And besides, Jessie hates going shopping too."

"Right." I stand up and tell her to have fun, then plunge into the pool. I exhale as I go down into the water, allowing myself to sink to the bottom, where I sit for as long as I can hold my breath. It's so silent and cool down here. So simple and calm. I wish I could stay like this forever. But suddenly my lungs are begging for oxygen, and I am forced to surface.

twenty

"PAY UP!" THE SOUND OF HIS VOICE PUMMELS INSIDE MY CHEST LIKE A bass drum. "*Pay up*, Hannah Johnson, or suffer forever!"

"I can't pay," I sob, hands clenched in front of me. My ankles are bound as I stand knee-deep in ice-cold water that is slimy and brown. Above me I see the tall, black podium where the judge is seated. I am naked and shivering, and I know that my fate is sealed.

The judge's face twists in rage, and his eyes are fiery red. His spiky black beard trembles as he shakes his golden gavel in the air. "*Pay up! Pay up!* Or suffer for eternity!"

"I have nothing to pay with," I confess.

"That's right!" he yells. "*You have nothing!* And yet you owe everything. *Pay up*, Hannah Johnson!"

"*Pay up!*" echoes the crowd that encircles me. All of them are fully dressed, and their faces are angry as they shake their fists in the air and scream at me. "*Pay up or pay the price!*"

"I can't!" I cry again and again. "I can't! I can't!"

And then I wake up in a cold sweat, the sheets twisted around me, my face wet with tears, and my heart racing. *Just a nightmare*, I tell myself as I take a deep breath and look at the clock. It's four a.m., and I'm wide-awake, the demand to "pay up!" still reverberating through my flustered head.

I get out of bed and pull on a robe, then open the door that leads to the little terrace outside my room. I'm still surprised at how the outside air is warmer than the inside as I sit in the rattan chair, pull my knees up to my chin, and just stare at the dark sky.

I tell myself that the dream is ridiculous, just my worried mind playing tricks on me. Maybe I do need therapy. But there is something about the scene that is eerily familiar too. Something that harkens back to the things I've heard over the years. Something spiritual.

But I know that the judge wasn't God. At least not the God I've always known or thought I knew. Although I'm not so sure any- more. I suppose I could have it all backward. I've gotten so much else backward since I came to the States. But no, I don't believe that judge was really God. And I don't believe that judge was the people I owe money to. Not sweet Uncle Ron or even Mr. Macy, whoever he may be.

And suddenly I know—I know without a doubt—that the cruel and vicious judge in my dream was the devil. Oh, perhaps not for real. But he was a symbol of the devil. And he wanted me to believe that I owed him something. And that I was going to suffer if I didn't pay. But I know this is ridiculous. Not to mention a big fat lie. And how do I know this? Because I know for a fact—in the same way that I know that the sun brings warmth and the rain fills the seas—that *Jesus already paid the debt*. I've known this for as long as I can remember. It wasn't his debt that he paid; it was mine. His death bought our forgiveness so that we won't suffer forever. How many times have I heard this preached?

But I don't think it's really hit home until now. It's a horrible feel- ing knowing that you're in over your head. That you've bought what you cannot pay for. That you owe more than you'll ever make. It's a hopeless, miserable, overwhelming feeling that makes you want to give up. And that's just money. What if it was your soul? Your peace? Your eternity?

"Oh, God," I say aloud—my first real prayer in weeks. "I am so sorry." I take in a deep breath as I consider the course of my life since leaving New Guinea, the way that I've played it fast and loose—both monetarily and spiritually. "I have been such a fool. Such a complete fool."

Then I get down on my knees and confess to God that I've blown it, that I've turned my back on him and turned my life into utter chaos. "I am spiritually bankrupt. I owe far more than I can ever pay." Then I ask God to forgive me. I ask him to take me back, make me part of his family again. And this time I know my heart is in this for real—and not because I've been pressured by church or family or the mission school. This time it's just Hannah Johnson and God—one on one—for the long haul. Somehow I know it. Something in me has changed.

I pray for a long time. So long that my knees are actually numb by the time I stand up. But as I stand, I feel that I've been scrubbed clean, that my debts really have been forgiven, and that life in me has been renewed. I lift my hands into the air and thank God, and I know, without a doubt, that life is going to be different from here on out.

Oh, sure, I know that I still have my bills to pay. But I also know that God is going to help me and strengthen me through the next couple of weeks until I'm finally able to break even. And I believe I'm going to do that—by the grace of God, *I'm going to do that*. And by the grace of God, I believe that I won't make these same mistakes again.

The sun is coming up now, and I decide that it's pointless to go back to bed. So I get dressed, go downstairs, and make coffee.

"What're you doing up this early on a Sunday?" asks Uncle Ron as he comes into the kitchen with newspaper in hand.

"Same to you," I say with a smile. "Want some coffee?"

He grins. "You and I, we must be related, huh?"

I nod and pour him a cup of coffee. "I reckon."

"Just don't turn into a workaholic like I am," he warns me as he sits down on the other side of the counter.

"I don't plan on it."

"Are you going back to your old hours next week?"

I consider this. "If you don't mind, I'd really like to keep up the long days for just two more weeks."

"Saving up for something special?" he asks. "Or just college?"

I feel my cheeks growing warm. "Not exactly," I say. Then I decide, even though it's humiliating, to just be honest. "I think I got in over my head," I admit.

"Over your head?" He frowns. "What do you mean? Don't tell me you've gotten into gambling." He grins now. "I've heard that's a problem with some of the employees. In fact, we're going to put something about it in the policy book this week."

I smile. "No, that's not it." Then I tell him about the Macy's card and how I blew almost my entire $2,000 draw on ridiculous clothes. "I don't know what came over me. I thought I had to dress like a celebrity or something."

He shakes his head. "I think I know what came over you. And they both live under this roof."

"No," I say quickly. "It's not their fault. Really. I made my own choices. I'm just not used to the lifestyle here. And I temporarily forgot that I'm not as wealthy as —"

Uncle Ron takes in a slow breath. "Without mentioning names, there are a couple of other people in this house who are having the same problem." He runs his fingers through his short-cropped hair. "And if they don't slow it down, we could be heading for trouble."

"Truly?"

He nods. "Not that I should be burdening you with this, Hannah. I've already talked to both of them and they don't seem to be taking me seriously. If I put a spending limit on one credit card, they just open another account. You should see the bills pouring in every month."

Now I feel even worse as I consider how Aunt Lori cosigned on my Macy's card. So I admit this to him. "But I'll have it completely paid off in two weeks," I promise him. "As well as what I owe you."

He laughs. "That's peanuts, Hannah. I mean, compared to what Lori and Vanessa have racked up in bills."

Then I tell him what Vanessa said about the Oprah show and how she thinks she might be a shopping addict. I know it might be wrong to snitch on her, but I reckon if she's really addicted, she might need help. He considers this. "You're probably on to something."

"Please don't tell her I told you."

"Don't worry. I had my suspicions already."

"Are you really in financial trouble?" I ask him, feeling truly concerned now.

He laughs but not with humor. "Oh, I don't know . . . the business is doing okay. But we're sure not as rich as Lori and Vanessa think. I wish those two would slow it down. And I do need to be putting more money away and back into the business, or we really could go belly-up. I guess it's up to me to put my foot down."

I feel sorry for him now. "I'm sure that won't be easy."

"Ever try to stop a moving freight train?"

I shake my head.

"You get the picture." Then he refills his coffee and excuses himself as he heads to his office to work, I'm sure. Maybe he is a workaholic. And maybe Aunt Lori and Vanessa are shopaholics. Maybe they all need therapy.

I plan to ring Jessie a little later when she's had time to wake up properly. I want to tell her about my dream and what happened early this morning. I reckon she'll understand. And who knows, maybe we can go surfing again someday.

I putter around the house, picking up in the kitchen since Consuela hasn't been in since Friday. Then I finally decide to ring Jessie. I'm all ready to leave her a message, but to my surprise, she actually answers the phone.

"Sorry for ringing you so early," I say quickly.

"No problem. I was just getting ready to go to church."

"Church?" I say the word as if it's something foreign to me.

"Remember?" she says. "That's the place where believers get together to worship God and stuff."

"Right." Then I laugh. "That sounds good."

"Sounds good?" she asks. "Meaning you'd like to go?"

"I reckon I would."

"Well, hold on to that thought, and I'll pick you up in about twenty minutes. Think you can be ready by then?"

"Sure."

So we hang up and I go upstairs to change my clothes. But as I stand there looking into my closet, I'm not even sure what Yanks wear to church. Back at the mission we usually dressed up a bit. But I recall seeing Jessie in trousers that time when she was just coming home from a service. Finally I decide on a white shirt, khaki skirt, and sandals—all from Ross Dress for Less. Boring perhaps, but at least these clothes are paid for. And if I'm going to worship God, I don't want to be distracted by nagging thoughts of debt.

As Jessie drives us to church, I tell her about my dream and recommitment to God.

"That's so cool," she says. "I've really been praying for you, Hannah. I sensed that God was working on you."

"Thanks," I tell her. "I really appreciate that." And I remember that Sophie has been praying for me too. I'll have to e-mail her and let her know that God was listening. I'm sure she'll be relieved, but knowing Sophie, she probably won't be surprised. For the first time it occurs to me that Sophie's faith has probably been more genuine than mine all along. Maybe because she came to God when she was older. Or maybe just because of the way God made her. But I think I will be better able to relate to her about spiritual things now. I feel as if my eyes have finally been opened.

As I sit through the service at Jessie's church, I can't believe how much I feel at home. It's completely different from the mission church I'm used to, and yet it's very similar too. I can't explain it. But somehow it feels deeply familiar, like a good friend you never realized you've always had. Like God.

Then a funny thing happens when they pass the collection plate around. I've already decided that I'm going to put in a twenty—a pretty big deal for me considering how stingy I've been lately. But I'm happy to give this money to God. And as I lay the bill in the plate, I notice the writing across the top—"In God We Trust"—and I am totally incredulous. And I wonder why I never noticed this before. What an amazing reminder for Yanks every time they pull money from their wallets. *In God we trust!* But so many, like me, seem to forget this or ignore it. Or perhaps they're not using cash but trusting in their Visa cards to carry them through. And then look what happens.

Anyway, I'm sure I'm grinning ear to ear by the time the service ends.

"What'd you think?" Jessie asks as we head to her car.

"Your church is awesome!"

"Cool. I hope you'll keep coming back."

"Me too. At least for the rest of the summer. I'm not really sure where we'll be after that."

"But I thought you were going to be here until December."

"We'll be in the country and probably in the LA area. But I don't know exactly where we'll live once my parents get back. You can be pretty sure it won't be in Orange County. A bit expensive for a missionary budget."

"That's too bad. I like having you around."

"Well, hopefully we can still get together sometimes." Even as I say this, I suspect it's unlikely because I won't have my own wheels after I leave Vanessa's family. Even so, I don't care. I would rather be poor with my own parents than have it all with Vanessa's. Not that I don't love Uncle Ron and Aunt Lori or that I don't totally appreciate their kindness and generosity, but their lifestyle's just a bit rich for my blood. I reckon living in the smallest village hut with my parents and being at peace would be good enough for me.

"You wanna surf today?" asks Jessie.

"I was hoping you'd ask."

So we stop by the house to get my beach bag and things, and it's barely past noon when we're out catching waves. Soon enough I am thinking about what Jessie told me—about how surfing is a form of worship for her. And next thing I know, I am praising God as I ride the curl of the wave with hands raised high. And I have never felt so free, so at peace, or so completely happy.

twenty-one

Iт's THE END OF AUGUST NOW. MY DEBTS ARE COMPLETELY PAID OFF, MY Macy's account is closed, and I have a bit of savings put aside. The girls at work had a little going-away party for me on my last day. And despite being tired of the whole office thing, I was sad to say good-bye.

"Want to go to Macy's for old time's sake?" asks Laticia. "There's a big sale today."

I laugh and say, "No thanks." By now I've confessed to them how I got in over my head in debt and how it's only by God's grace that I didn't go totally bonkers before I climbed out of the hole. And I think they understood.

My parents are back and staying at Uncle Ron's until they can find a place to rent for a few months. It's Saturday afternoon and we're all hanging out by the pool, which my parents have put to as much good use as I've managed to do. The funny thing is that Uncle Ron and Aunt Lori have been swimming in it lately too. And I think they're actually enjoying it. Not only that, but my dad and uncle even played golf today. I reckon Uncle Ron might be trying to reform his workaholic ways. Or maybe he's just taking an obligatory vacation. In any case, I hope he enjoys himself enough to break away more often.

"Someone from the main office has an apartment they're willing to sublet until the New Year," my dad's telling Aunt Lori. She's just inquired about how far away we'd be once we settle in for the duration of our furlough. I actually think she might miss us once we move on. She's spent the entire week with Mum and even postponed her hair appointment until after we leave. "It's north of LA. Not the best neighborhood, but the rent is affordable." Dad winks at me now. "Or we could just camp out in the Taurus. I'm sure Hannah wouldn't mind a bit."

"Not if you camped near a good surfing location," I toss back at him from where I'm toweling dry on the deck. "We could all become beach bums and I could surf the time away. I'm pretty sure Jessie would loan me her board again."

"Speaking of Jessie," says Vanessa suddenly, "she called here while you and your mom were out this afternoon. She'd been trying to reach you on your cell, but I told her you had it cancelled because you thought it was an unnecessary expense. It sounded pretty urgent though, and I promised her I'd have you call her right back."

So I excuse myself and go inside to use the phone. I feel concerned as I dial the number. I hope nothing is wrong.

"Vanessa said to ring you," I say quickly when she answers. "She said it was urgent."

"Oh, good!" she exclaims. "Have your parents signed any leases yet?"

"Huh?"

"You know, for where you're going to live. Have they done anything—"

"I don't think so. But Dad's got a place he's going to look at tomorrow. Some apartment north of LA."

"Well, how about this idea? You see, I was talking to my dad yesterday. By the way, he thinks you're a very nice girl."

"Uh, thanks." I'm not exactly sure what that means. But I did have an interesting conversation with Mr. VanHorn one afternoon when he popped into the beach house a week or so ago. He caught me cleaning up in the kitchen and naturally assumed I was the housekeeper, but then I explained, and we chatted a bit until Jessie came down from her shower.

"Anyway, I told my dad how your parents are missionaries and how you're looking for a place to live and he said, 'Why don't you invite them to stay at the beach house until January?'"

"Really?"

"Yeah. I was a little surprised myself. But then, Dad and Carrie will be in Maui for about six weeks this fall—our grandmother's coming to stay with us. And I suspect he thinks if the beach house is occupied by respectable, clean-living, missionary-type folks, it will not only keep Felicia from having any more wild parties, but it might prevent break-ins as well. That happens a lot when beach houses are left vacant for too long. You know Daddy, always thinking of ways to help others." She laughs and I know she's making a joke.

"That's very generous of him, Jessie."

"Yeah, it is, isn't it?"

"But do you really think he's serious? I mean, we can't afford—"

"No, he doesn't want any rent. Just responsible house sitters, you know. Of course, he wants to meet your parents first. But do you think they'd be interested?"

"Are you kidding?" Then she tells me his number and I promise to have my dad give him a call.

I can hardly believe it when I hang up the phone. And my parents can hardly believe it when I tell them. But then my dad just smiles and says, "See, it's like I'm always saying, the good Lord provides. You just have to trust him."

Now, I might not have agreed with him a few months ago, but today I think Dad is right. God does provide, and you do have to trust. As soon as you start running ahead and grabbing stuff up for yourself, you're sure to end up in a mess. And while I know I'm not immune to messes, I reckon I can avoid a few bungles by following God's lead.

All in all, I think this summer has been a relatively cheap lesson for me. Oh, I'll admit it felt pretty costly when I was in the thick of it. But about a week ago, I overheard Uncle Ron telling Aunt Lori and Vanessa exactly how much money they'd spent in the last six months—apparently he tallied it all up. I really didn't mean to eavesdrop, but I was just getting a soft drink from the fridge while he was giving them what for in his office. And he shouted out the amount in a voice loud enough that I'm sure the neighbors heard too. And the total was truly staggering. In fact, it was even more money than it takes to support my parents in their missions work for an entire year. And all I could think was, *What a waste. What a sad and pitiful waste.*

Of course, I will never broadcast those details to anyone. But I will be praying for their family. All in all, I have great hope. And I'd rather put my trust in God than in money any day of the week.

reader's guide

1. Before coming to the States, Hannah was never too concerned with money or material things. What caused her values to change?

2. Why do you think Vanessa had such a need to buy only the "best" and most expensive clothes?

3. Aunt Lori and Vanessa had no concern about using credit for their purchases. What do you think about buying things with credit cards?

4. Why do you think Hannah left her Bible behind when she came to the States?

5. What do you think causes a person to become a "shopaholic"?

6. How do you think America's values in regard to money and materialism compare to other countries' values? Explain.

7. What did you think of Wyatt? What was important to him in life? Why? Do you support his motivation?

8. Hannah felt trapped by her debt. How do you feel when you owe someone something? How would you feel if you owed more than you could pay?

9. Jessie seemed pretty well-grounded for a "rich" girl. Why do you think that was?

10. Hannah was surprised to read "In God We Trust" on the United States' money. How do you feel when you see those words?

TrueColors Book 7:

Blade Silver

Coming in October 2005

All I'm looking for is a little harmless relief from the pain.

One

SOMETIMES I FEEL LIKE I'M ABOUT TO EXPLODE. OR MAYBE I WILL implode. I'm not really sure, but I think it's going to get messy. And I think someone's going to get hurt. Probably me.

I turn my CD player up a couple of notches. Not loud enough to attract his attention—I don't want that—but loud enough to drown out his voice as he rages at my fourteen-year-old brother. I'd like to stand up for Caleb. I even try to imagine myself going out there and bravely speaking out in my younger brother's defense. But the problem is, I'm just a big chicken.

Besides that, I know what will happen if I try to tell Dad that it's not Caleb's fault, if I try to explain that Mom forgot to give us lunch money again today and that Caleb was just trying to get by. But I can tell by the volume of Dad's voice that it's already too late to reason with him. And while I can't discern his exact words over the sound of Avril Lavigne's lyrics, I can feel them cutting and slicing through Caleb—and me.

I imagine my younger brother shredded and bleeding out there. A big red puddle spilled out across the pale yellow vinyl in our kitchen.

My dad never hits us with his fists. He never slaps us around or takes off his belt. He would be too concerned about leaving welts or bruises, something that someone might notice. But his words are worse than a beating. And they leave invisible scars—scars that never seem to fade.

Finally it gets quiet out there. I hear Caleb's bedroom door, across the hall from mine, closing quietly. He knows not to slam it. That would only prolong the agony. And after a bit, I hear the door to the garage bang shut and then the sound of my dad's Ford diesel truck roaring down the driveway and onto the road.

It's safe to go out now, but I still feel guilty for not defending Caleb. I creep out and stand in the hallway, hovering like a criminal in front of his door, my hand poised to knock softly, ready to go in and tell him I understand how he feels and that I'm sorry. But I can hear him crying now. And I can hear him punching something. It sounds like his pillow or maybe his mattress—*pow pow pow*, again and again—and I know that if I try to say something to him while he's like this, I'll only make things worse.

The last time I tried to comfort him, he got seriously angry at me. He told me that I don't understand anything. He said that Dad might come down on me sometimes, but it's never as bad as with him. "You're Dad's favorite," he finally spat, slamming his door right in my face. So I know better than to say anything when he's feeling this mad. But it worries me. What if he becomes like Dad? What if the day comes when I can't even talk to him?

I look at the closed door at the end of the hallway. My parents' bedroom. Mom is in there. I can hear strains of that obnoxious *Jeopardy* theme music coming quietly from her little TV. It's her favorite show, and when she's feeling good, she can get most of the answers right. But that won't be the case tonight. She's been in one of her "down" moods for several weeks now. No telling how long this one will last.

As much as I hate to disturb her when she's like this, I know this is my best chance to ask her for lunch money—for both me and Caleb. Either that or I'll have to see if there's anything in the kitchen that I can use to make us lunches for tomorrow. But somehow I have to make sure that Caleb does not have to borrow money from anyone at school tomorrow. I don't know why he went and bummed lunch money from Sally today.

Sally is our first cousin. Her family lives in a nice neighborhood a couple of miles from here, and although she may be good to loan out a buck or two, Caleb should've known she'd tell her dad (who is our dad's older brother) and that Uncle Garrett would call our dad and teasingly ask why Caleb was begging money from his Sally today. That's what ignited our dad's fuse tonight. But in all fairness to Caleb, if it hadn't been the lunch money, it would've been something else. The trash still sitting out on the street, a bike parked in the front yard, shoes left on the floor in the living room—it doesn't take much. He went ballistic one night last week because someone had left the hose running. Turned out it was him. But he never apologized.

His solution, after a tirade, is to leave here mad. And we all know that he goes to one of two places. He wants us to think he's at his friend Jimmy's, where they mess around with the restoration of an old Corvette and drink beer. But we also know that he spends a fair amount of time at The Dark Horse. It's a sleazy-looking bar in one of the alleys downtown. He parks his pickup in the back and hangs out there until he's forgotten whatever it was that made him so angry.

Dysfunctional? Well, duh. But most people looking at our family from the outside are totally clueless. Including Dad's best friend, Jimmy, and even Uncle Garrett. Despite Uncle Garrett's flaws, I'm sure he has no idea that his younger brother has such an anger problem. Most people who know my dad think he's the nicest guy in town. He manages Jackson's Tire Company and always has a ready smile or a goofy joke for anyone—anyone who doesn't live inside this house, that is. And I'm sure that everyone just looks at our family and assumes that everything's fine and dandy. We are all so very good at keeping up appearances.

But what am I supposed to do with all this pain? I mean, I've got Caleb across the hall, crying and swearing and pounding on things. I've got my mom holed up in her room, eyes glazed over by Xanax, I'm sure, as she sits in the little gliding rocker next to her bed and just stares at the tiny TV that sits on her bureau.

Instead of returning to my room, I go into the bathroom that Caleb and I have to share. We do our best not to fight over it, like some of my friends do with their brothers—at least not while Dad is around. I sigh as I look into the mirror above the bathroom sink. My face, as usual, is expressionless. Although my eyes could give me away, if anyone really looked. To me they are two black holes. A constant reminder of the deep hopelessness of my life. I push a strand of straight dark hair out of my face. I've been growing my bangs out lately, and they've reached that place where they're just in the way. Sort of like me.

It won't be long until I'm out of this madhouse for good. Recently I've been playing with the idea of graduating a year early, getting out of here when I'm only seventeen. I've heard it can be done.

The question is, can I really last that long? Every single day I tell myself I'm not going to do this thing again. I'm not going to give into it one more time. And some days I actually succeed. But on other days, like today, it is impossible. The tightness inside my chest is painful right now. And I wonder if a fairly healthy sixteen-year-old can have a heart attack. Maybe that would be the answer.

For no particular reason, other than habit, I turn on the tap water and let it just run into the sink. It's how I usually do this thing. Maybe the sound is meant to camouflage what's really going on in here. I don't know. Or maybe it's comforting to watch the water flowing. I just stand there and watch it run. I don't wash my hands, or brush my teeth, or wash my face. I simply stand there with hands planted on either side of the sink, as I lean forward and stare at the water flowing from the faucet and going down the drain. I'm sure my dad would think this is stupid and wasteful. I'm sure if I ever got caught, I would get quite a lecture on just how much he pays for the water and electric bill every month. And normally, I do try to be frugal, but there are times like now when I really don't care.

I don't know how long I stand there wasting valuable water, but finally I turn off the faucet and take in a deep breath. I wish I could stop doing this, but I still have this ache inside. Instead of diminishing, it only seems to grow—pushing and pushing against my insides until I don't see how I can contain it anymore.

I open the bottom drawer on my side of the bathroom cabinet. It's where I keep my "feminine" products—a place I can be certain that my dad or brother would never go looking. And my mother, well, she would never think to go looking for anything of mine in

219

the first place. She can hardly find her slippers in the morning.

I take out a box of tampons and turn it over to see a sliver of silver glinting from where the cardboard overlaps on the bottom. I carefully slide out the blade and hold it between my thumb and forefinger. It's an old-fashioned, two-sided kind of blade. I swiped one from Caleb when he first started shaving with my grandpa's old razor set. It didn't take my little brother very long to realize that there are better shaving instruments available, and he never seems to notice when a blade goes missing out of the little cardboard box alongside the old brass razor. Not that I've had to replace many blades during these past six months. As long as you wash and dry them and keep them in a safe place, they can last quite a while.

At first I thought I would limit my cutting to my left arm. But after a few weeks, I started running out of places to cut. And that's when I realized I'm fairly coordinated at cutting with my left hand. My right arm has a series of evenly spaced stripes to prove this. I push up the sleeve of my shirt and examine the stripes with routine interest, running my fingers over the ones that are healed and barely touching the ones that are still tender. Each one could tell a story. Okay, the stories would be pretty similar, but each scar is unique. I made my most recent one only two days ago. It's still pretty sore.

Already I am beginning to feel relief. I have no idea why this is. But it's always like this. Just the security of holding the blade in my hand, just knowing that I am in control now, is almost enough. But not quite.

I lower the blade to the pale white skin on the inside of my arm, and using a sharp corner of the blade, I quickly make about a two-inch slash. I know not to go too deep. And when I'm in control, like now, I can do it just right. And just like that, I'm done. I hardly feel the pain of the cut anymore. It's like it doesn't even hurt.

I watch with familiar fascination as the blood oozes out in a clean, straight line. There is something so reassuring about seeing my bright red blood exposed like this. It's like this sign that I'm still alive and, weird as it sounds, that someday everything will be okay. And although the euphoria that follows the cut never lasts as long as I wish it would, it's a quick fix that mostly works.

I press a wad of toilet paper on the wound. For the moment, this cut will absorb all my attention and emotional energy. It will block out what I am unable to deal with. And for a while, it will convince me that I will actually survive my life.

Am I proud of my behavior? Of course not. But hey, this isn't as bad as doing drugs, like some of my friends do. Or getting drunk, like my dad is doing right now. Or just checking out, like my mom did last year and continues to do on an off-and-on basis.

Even so, it's my dirty little secret, and for the time being, it's all I have to keep me from falling. So don't judge me.

about the author

MELODY CARLSON has written dozens of books for all age groups, but she particularly enjoys writing for teens. Perhaps this is because her own teen years remain so vivid in her memory. After claiming to be an atheist at the ripe old age of twelve, she later surrendered her heart to Jesus and has been following him ever since. Her hope and prayer for all her readers is that each one would be touched by God in a special way through her stories. For more information, please visit Melody's website at www.melodycarlson.com.